THE BIG DIRT NAP

Also by Rosemary Harris

Pushing Up Daisies

THE
BIG DIRT NAP

A Dirty Business

Mystery

Rosemary Harris

 Minotaur Books ✖ New York

For Bruce and Paula,

who continue to inspire me

A THOMAS DUNNE BOOK FOR MINOTAUR BOOKS.
An imprint of St. Martin's Publishing Group.

THE BIG DIRT NAP. Copyright © 2009 by Rosemary Harris. All rights reserved. Printed in the United States of America. For information, address St. Martin's Press, 175 Fifth Avenue, New York, N.Y. 10010.

www.thomasdunnebooks.com
www.minotaurbooks.com

library of Congress Cataloging-in-Publication Data

Harris, Rosemary.
    The big dirt nap : a dirty business mystery / Rosemary Harris. — 1st ed.
        p. cm.
ISBN-13: 978-0-312-36968-2
ISBN-10: 0-312-36968-9
    1. Women gardeners—Fiction.   2. Casinos—Connecticut—Fiction.
3. Connecticut—Fiction.   I. Title.
    PS3608.A78328B54 2009
    813'.6—dc22

                                                            2008033955

First Edition: February 2009

10 9 8 7 6 5 4 3 2 1

Acknowledgments

To all the booksellers who welcomed me and made a newcomer feel like an old pro, especially Barbara Peters, Mary Alice Gorman, Maggie Topkis, Roberta Rubin, Mitch Kaplan, Dianne Defonce, and Sharon Roth. To the dedicated librarians—one of whom was kind enough to say that I must have been a librarian in a previous life—especially to my friends in Stamford, Fairfield, New Canaan, Darien, Westport, Newington, Forestville, Easton, and Milford, Connecticut, and to my friends in Princeton and Hunterdon, New Jersey, and in Cary, North Carolina.

Special thanks to Suzanne Wickham, Kim Hicks, Hector DeJean, Monica Katz, and Talia Ross for looking after me.

Dirt Nap—n. a state of permanent rest, death, as in *taking the big dirt nap.*

One

Maybe I'd have had a drink with the guy if I had known the next time I saw him he'd be sprawled out in a Dumpster enclosure, with a greasy newspaper tented over his face. Then again, maybe not.

Nick Vigoriti had unsuccessfully hit on me as I sipped club soda at the bar. There were two or three likelier candidates in skimpier outfits who weren't working on a laptop, but he zeroed in on me.

I knew him, sort of. Earlier in the day, Vigoriti had been on line behind me checking into the Titans Hotel in Connecticut's wine country. We'd spent what seemed like twenty minutes listening to a statuesque redhead spitting out demands and fidgeting almost as much as the white Maltese she carried in her plastic designer bag.

"That is not friendly."

The pimply kid behind the reception desk nodded furiously.

That, combined with the oversize jacket that hopefully fit his night-shift counterpart better, gave him the appearance of a life-size bobble-head doll.

"April does not need a sitter. I only came to this establishment because it's supposed to be pet-friendly. I could have gotten comped at Hunting Ridge." She towered over the poor kid, the pile of hair on her head giving her an extra four inches, as if she needed it.

Vigoriti and I exchanged brief "whaddya gonna do" glances, until the dog's owner finished tormenting the desk clerk, then teetered off accompanied by a full luggage cart and the only bell-man in sight.

When it was my turn, I set my backpack on the counter, leaned over, and told the clerk my name.

"I don't see you," he said, scrolling down the computer screen. He forced himself to say the words, anticipating another pain-in-the-neck customer. Beads of sweat popped up on his forehead like condensation on a glass. I felt for the guy; he was getting a crash course in Difficult Guests 101 on what I was guessing was his first week on the job. "I'm sorry," he said, his voice cracking. "Did you make the reservation online, by any chance?"

Great. I'd sat through rush-hour traffic on the highway and now there was no room at the inn. "It has to be there," I said, trying not to betray my real feelings. "Will you please look again?"

He continued to scan the screen; then it occurred to me that my friend Lucy had made the reservation. Maybe it was under her name or her company's.

"Can you check under KCPS-TV? Or Cavanaugh. Check *Cavanaugh*," I repeated, louder, in that stupid way people do when they're talking to foreigners, as if saying something louder is going to make it easier to understand.

"Okay, okay, I got it. Here it is. 'Two adults, two doubles, no pets,' " he read off the screen. Relief washed over the kid's face; he didn't need another guest with problems. This job was already an interruption of his real life—which was probably football, getting good grades, and procuring the perfect fake ID, not standing in a gold-braided uniform two sizes too big and catching verbal abuse. I didn't blame him; I was in a service business myself and sometimes it wore thin.

I gave him my credit card for the "incidentals" and watched as he mindlessly swiped it and handed it back without even checking my name or the photo on the front.

"I'll just need one key. My friend will be joining me later." I plucked the paper folder from the counter and slid one plastic key back to him.

"Thank you, Ms. Cavanaugh."

I started to correct him, then thought, *What's the point?*

"You're welcome." I snatched my bag from the counter and turned to leave. Asking him where the elevators were would only have extended the experience, so I went off in the same direction as the woman with the dog. I was hardly going to get lost in a suburban Connecticut hotel.

On the way, smack in the middle of the lobby, was an octagonal enclosure about twenty feet wide. Inside it, in a huge terracotta pot, was the reason I was there. Well, one of them anyway. Inside the glass enclosure was a corpse flower. I moved in for a closer look, setting my things down briefly on one of the laminated benches that circled the glass gazebo.

The pot itself was about four feet in diameter, and shooting straight up from the center was a light green veined shaft tinged with purplish pink. I hadn't seen one in a few years and there was no getting around it—with that color and that shape . . .

"Pretty sexy if you ask me," Vigoriti had said, over my shoulder.

"I didn't ask you," I said, firmly enough to let him know I wasn't about to engage in a junior-high-school-level conversation regarding a certain part of the male anatomy. Not with a stranger anyway.

I picked up my bags, headed back toward the bank of elevators, around the corner from reception, and made a beeline for the first white triangle pointing up. Once inside, I pushed the button for my floor and crumpled, exhausted, against the side of the car. Just as the doors were closing, a hand slapped them apart.

The hand was an unlikely combination of manicured and rough, as if a boxer had buffed his nails. A black leather strap was twisted around the thick wrist and the large tanned hand held, of all things, a man bag, almost lost in its owner's large palm. The shirtsleeve was rolled up, thin gray stripes on black silk. Expensive, but not top of the line. And it half covered the muscular forearm of Nick Vigoriti.

"Hello, again." He smiled, pushed the doors open, and settled politely into the opposite corner of the car. I could tell he was looking at me, but I pretended not to notice.

Vigoriti gave off the very appealing scent of whiskey, sweat, and, if I remembered correctly from two boyfriends ago, a dash of Armani—ordinarily a winning trifecta and one I'd succumbed to in the past. But I was tired from the long drive and wasn't feeling particularly friendly. Besides, this was an all-girls weekend. Lucy and I each had work to do, but it was really about two old friends catching up. I flashed him the fake one-second, toothless smile you use to acknowledge someone's existence, then fixed my gaze straight ahead at the diamond pattern on the wall of the elevator until six pings told me I'd reached my floor. Vigoriti got out, too.

For an instant, my antenna went up, but he turned left before I'd committed to either direction. Happily, my room was on the right and I rushed down the hall, shifting my bags to one side and trying to remember which pocket I'd stuck the room key in.

I fished the plastic card out of its sheath and slipped it into the lock. Nothing. I tried it stripe up, stripe down, toward me, and away from me. Five minutes later, after repeated wipes against my sweatshirt, the uncooperative sliver of plastic still refused to admit me to my room. I sank my forehead against the door and let out a low groan like a wounded animal.

"They're a pain, aren't they?" Vigoriti said, standing over my shoulder.

I hadn't heard him approach, and was so startled I bumped my head looking up. Assessing the damage with one hand, I gave him the key with the other. "I'm not proud. You try."

He dipped the key once and the light flashed green.

"How did you do that?"

"Magnetism. You have to have a magnetic personality."

He had spared me a return match with the sweet but dopey desk clerk, so I resisted the urge to snort at his lame come-on.

"I'm kidding," he said. "Sometimes technology just likes to . . . *mess* with you." He held on to the key a few seconds longer than necessary, slapping it against his palm. Then he blew on it—as if to blow imaginary cooties away—and handed it back to me.

I picked up my bags, held the door open just a crack with my hip, and waited for him to leave. "Thanks," I said, hoping he'd take the hint.

He shrugged and strode down the hall to the elevators. Trailing him, in the air with his pheromones, was the word he almost said, but didn't. *Fuggedaboudit.*

I wouldn't have been at Titans at all if Lucy Cavanaugh hadn't lured me there at the last minute with the offer of a free room, a spa weekend, and the promise of a corpse flower just about to bloom. Any one of those might have done the trick, but all three were irresistible. And I needed to believe I still did things spontaneously.

I'd gotten freebies all the time in my old television job, but they were few and far between since I'd started Dirty Business a couple of years back. Dirty Business was going through the terrible twos—sometimes wonderful and sometimes not. This was one of the *not* periods—before the season started, when I was planning my year but some of my clients still had holiday wreaths on their front doors. I had jumped at the chance for a few days of rest and relaxation on someone else's dime. Once I knew we were going to Titans, I managed to squeeze a few bucks and a byline out of my local paper to let me write a piece on the rare corpse flower on display at the hotel. If nothing else it would get my name out in front of potential clients.

Lucy was venturing outside of New York City to chase down a story for *Sin in Suburbia,* a cable series I'd inadvertently helped her start a year ago. The series had seemed like a good idea at the time and the network had ordered more episodes, but it hadn't initially registered with Lucy that she'd actually have to spend time in the suburbs, and that was tough duty for a woman who got vertigo anytime she went farther north.

If we hadn't planned to meet at the bar I'd have been in bed with room service and the remote, and I'd have saved my picture taking until the morning. As it was, I swapped my sneakers for short cowboy boots and my T-shirt for a plain white shirt, which I tucked into my jeans. With a not-too-out-of-style dark blazer and a little bronzer I convinced myself I looked professional, French—simple and elegant.

Not that Titans had anything remotely like a dress code—the

few people I had seen when I checked in could have been going to a kids' soccer game. But I spent most of my days in gardening gear—pants tucked into socks to avoid ticks, baggy long-sleeved tops to avoid scratches, and when necessary a white mesh bug suit that covered me from head to toe and made me look like something out of a 1950s horror movie about the aftereffects of the hydrogen bomb. I welcomed any occasion to clean up my act.

An hour later, after taking more than two dozen pictures of the corpse flower, I was at the bar nursing my third club soda, feeling bloated and losing patience. There was a grand piano in the bar but judging by the amount of dust on it I didn't think I was in for any live music. I tried to ignore the third Muzak go-round of that weepy song from *Titanic* and passed the time by filling in the details for the corpse flower story. I Googled the hotel's history and checked out the clientele. No one was paying any attention to the plant. The seven-foot object in the glass box might have been a priceless sculpture or a giant turd for all anyone at Titans seemed to care. I scoured the room for someone to interview but the pickings were slim: a few Asian guys, a skinny blonde reading a romance novel, and a twitchy guy who looked like he desperately needed a drink. Then I saw *him* again.

Vigoriti entered the raised bar area and surveyed the place as if he owned it. He unwrapped a candy and popped it in his mouth, tossing the wrapper at a nearby ashtray and missing. I hoped he wouldn't notice me or would have the good sense to realize I wasn't interested, but my limited experience with him already told me what to expect. Uninvited, he slid onto the bar stool right next to me.

"You going gambling? If you're calculating the odds on that computer I can tell you they always favor the house," he said, his breath first-date minty. He must have been joking with that line.

This time I took a better look at him. He was handsome in a banged-up, been-around-the-block way. Built like a quarterback, or at least what they look like with all the padding—big shoulders, small hips. And he had great hair. Long, but intellectual long, not aging-record-business-skinny-ponytail *what are you thinking?* long. Then there was that intoxicating scent. There was no denying it, Nick Vigoriti smelled like trouble, or at the very least, an adventure. And I hadn't had one lately.

"No kidding," I said, snapping out of his thrall. "And is that your finding after years of careful research?" I flipped the computer screen halfway down.

"I just got back from Vegas," he said. "Thought I'd save you some dough."

"I'm waiting for a friend," I said, hoping to head him off *before* the pass.

"Could be I'm that friend."

He was losing points rapidly. Good looks got you so far with me, but a guy needed to have some gray matter. "Do you get many takers with these lines?" I asked.

"Depends. On how young they are, how smart they are," he said, smiling and eyeing the other women at the bar. He turned back to me. "Now, those girls are girls. I'm looking for a woman, about thirty to thirty-five, long dark hair, athletic build," he said, giving a pretty good description of me.

I held up my hands to stop him. "I'm going to give you the benefit of the doubt. This may not even be where you're going, but I'm not looking for a good time. Not that kind of good time. I'm waiting for a friend. A real one, not one who's in town for the widget convention. And *she's* late. Other than her, the only reason I'm here is the titan arum," I said, attempting to scare him off with a little Latin. "The corpse flower." I motioned in its direction.

"Corpse flower? Is that what they call that stinkweed in the glass box?"

He pointed to the plant we'd been looking at earlier, the titan arum, the largest unbranched inflorescence in the world. In simple terms, the biggest flower that isn't on a tree. Spectacular and rare, but unsettling, since the corpse flower looks like a giant phallus, and smells, well, like rotting meat; hence the name, and the need for an enclosure. I was guessing some dumb schmuck who didn't know any better thought the titan arum would be a clever promotion for Titans. I was also guessing same dumb schmuck was currently looking for another job.

"I heard the Mishkins had to fork over five grand for that box," he said, "to keep the stench away from the paying customers. And they're probably going to trash it once the damn thing blooms and it's shipped back to the jungle."

"I doubt they'll do that. Smarter to donate it and get the tax deduction. The University of Wisconsin has a few corpse flowers. I'm sure UConn would love to have it; theirs bloomed a few years ago." He eyed me as if I'd just spoken in tongues or cracked the human genome. Okay, he wasn't into plants . . . or big words. But the longer I looked at him, the less I cared. Brains weren't everything, and anyway, we were just talking.

If I stuck to club soda and we stayed in safe territory conversationwise, he could stay. Besides, I'd enjoy the look on Lucy's face when she rushed in breathlessly with stories and apologies and saw me sitting with a sexy beast like Nick Vigoriti. She and the rest of my friends had been after me to start dating again ever since I left New York City, and this little encounter might shut them up for a while. He might even contribute something interesting about the hotel that I could use for the article. Who knew?

"Who are the Mishkins?" I asked, surreptitiously keying that info into the laptop.

"Bernie Mishkin and his sister," he said, watching me use the computer. "Are you writing this down now?"

"Yeah. Is that a problem?"

Vigoriti shrugged. "Same difference. The Mishkins own the place," he said, waving the sad-eyed bartender over. "They and their numerous partners."

The bartender had a heart-shaped face and lank hair that hung in a skinny braid halfway down her back.

"What're you having, Nicky?" she asked, in an accent I couldn't initially place, then decided was Russian. She wiped nonexistent spills from the bar and slipped a coaster in front of him, grazing his fingers.

"Dirty martini," he said, pulling back his hand. "You?" he asked me.

Every stupid thing I'd done in my adult life had come after a few drinks, and I could imagine getting very stupid with Nick Vigoriti, so I stuck with club soda.

"Can you introduce me to them?" I asked. "The Mishkins?"

"You think that's a good idea?"

"Why not?" I said. "I may have a lucrative proposition for them."

"They're always interested in money." He laughed. "I haven't talked to Bernie for a while, but that may change. His wife died a few months back. I haven't seen much of him since then. . . . I was really friendlier with her."

Why was I not surprised? What woman wouldn't want to be friends with a handsome stud who hung on your every word and made you feel as if you were the only woman in the room worth talking to?

The bartender brought our drinks. Nick's had six green olives on two plastic toothpicks. The bartender moved off to another customer but not before giving me a look that suggested she wouldn't mind seeing my head on a sharpened stick.

"What did *I* do?"

"Oksana's a good kid," he said, swallowing hard and nodding in her direction.

"Adorable."

"I used to work here," Vigoriti continued. "Before Mishkin brought in the Malaysians, the Ukranians, let's see . . ." He rattled off a laundry list of ethnic groups, then took a long pull on his drink. "Who is it now, Oksana?" he called out to the bartender.

"Chinese, I think," she said, over her shoulder, already fixing him a second drink.

"Their board meetings must look like a Benetton ad," I muttered.

"Most of them cut bait."

"It doesn't look like business is too bad; there are people here," I said.

"We could go somewhere private to discuss this," he said, signaling Oksana that he was ready for round two. He polished off his drink and slid all the olives into his mouth in a surprisingly suggestive move that made me rethink how friendly I wanted to appear.

"You know, I was just trying to be polite. Always dangerous at a bar. I'm sorry if I misled you, but I really am waiting for someone, and it isn't you." As if on cue, my phone beeped with a text message. Lucy was running late. Typical. She'd gotten a late start to begin with and one of the cheap Chinese New York-to-Boston shuttle buses had collided with a construction-materials truck. Gravel was spread all over I-95. The result was the same as if a load of ball bearings had spilled out on the highway; cars were drifting side to side as if they were in a Japanese video game. Lucy was stuck on the road, near Stamford, and wrote that she'd call when she got closer.

Locals were trickling into the bar for after-dinner drinks, working guys with puffy baseball caps. And businessmen who might have heard about the mess on 95 and preferred to sit here instead of in traffic. I debated the pros and cons of staying at the bar with Nick and possibly moving on to the harder stuff but decided against it. Life was complicated enough.

I chugged my drink and shut down the computer. "I'm gonna cut bait, to use your expression. I have to go. I was serious about meeting the Mishkins, though. I may have a buyer." I whipped out my business card and handed it to Nick as I got up to leave. He looked puzzled and studied the card for longer than it took to read the six or eight words on it. Was it possible the guy couldn't read? "For the greenhouse," I said, "the glass enclosure?"

A smile crept over Nick's handsome face.

"What's so funny?"

"My mistake," he said, flicking the card with his index finger. "Not the kind of dirt I thought you dug up."

That's how my business card came to be in the breast pocket of his shirt, and that's why the cops called on me hours later to identify his body.

I'm a gardener. Paula Holliday, sole proprietor of Dirty Business, garden design, container maintenance, and the occasional exhumation. Not really, although that was the way my last major landscaping job turned out, in Springfield, Connecticut, where I live, about seventy miles south of the Titans Hotel.

Titans had been built in the twenties, a place where businessmen parked their families for the summer and raced up to on Friday afternoons. Third-tier comics and wedding and bar mitzvah bands played there on the weekends. The men would bake themselves with sun reflectors, drink heavily, and have their conjugal visits. Then they'd wake up at the crack of dawn on Mondays, speeding back to Boston or New York and clocking themselves so they could compare travel times over drinks the following Friday.

By the sixties and seventies, kids didn't want to vacation with their parents anymore, Mom was just as likely to be working as Dad, and lots of hotels like Titans fell to the wrecking ball. Somehow Titans had survived. That was as far as my online research had gotten me before Nick joined me at the bar.

I got to the elevator just as April, the white Maltese, and her redheaded owner were exiting, the larger of the two in a skintight tangerine outfit with hot-pink trim that accentuated her big frame. The woman looked away quickly, and I watched her make her way to the taxi line in front of the hotel, the scrawny dog hurrying to keep up.

Maybe some of Nick's magnetism had rubbed off because, upstairs, this time my key card worked perfectly. The suite Lucy had reserved for us was large and benignly ugly. Nothing atrocious, just endless swathes of beige and dusty pink, from the synthetic bedspread and carpet, harboring god-knew-what kind of microorganisms, to the particleboard furniture. The only good news was that the furniture was from the sixties or seventies, so old there was an excellent chance that all of the formaldehyde had already been thrown off.

I hung the DO NOT DISTURB sign on the doorknob and automatically turned on the television, something I always do in hotel rooms, but rarely do at home. A hotel channel reminiscent of the cheap ads at movie theaters showed slides of the lobby and a kidney-shaped pool that must have been another vestige from Titans's good old days. The local news featured repeated helicopter shots of the collision on 95 from the same two angles. I kept the news on to get an update as to when Lucy might arrive and unpacked the rest of my things.

After years of traveling for work, I was an expert at packing light. Now that I rarely needed to look like a grown-up, I was even better at it. The white shirt went everywhere with me, and black jeans and a black jacket could pass for business attire if I needed to look reasonably professional. That was my uniform. I'd thrown a pair of low-rise yoga pants and a thin hoodie into the bag and that was what I climbed into.

The Titans room-service menu was almost as limited as my wardrobe and my viewing options, but I settled on a turkey club, hoping that the tryptophan would counteract the caffeine in the diet sodas I'd guzzled on the drive to Titans. Then I curled up on the scratchy synthetic love seat and waited for food and Lucy.

I should have been at home fine-tuning this year's plan for Caroline Sturgis's garden. Dirty Business had a few customers in the high-rent district, and a handful of retailers whose seasonal planters I serviced, but Caroline was my biggest and favorite individual client. Four and a half rolling acres bordering the arboretum, money to burn, and always happy to see me. And she had so much lawn that her property was like a blank slate, like that chunky brick of loose-leaf paper the first week of school. Filled with possibilities.

No matter how hard I tried, I couldn't entirely quash her enthusiasm for a green carpet and mass plantings of monochromatic annuals and bulbs. But I was chipping away at her, and her lawn, and had arranged to see her later that week. I wanted to be armed with sketches and some innovative ideas for her garden. That's what I should have been doing, instead of sitting in a monastic room with mediocre food and no cable.

I must have dozed off on the love seat around nine P.M. and the knock came not long after. Still in my flip-flops, yoga pants, and hoodie, I opened my door and was then led downstairs and through the lobby by two uniformed cops and a hotel security guard who had introduced himself as Hector Ruiz. Hector was as short and wide as my first car, a vintage Volkswagen Rabbit. Remarkably, the shiny suit he wore was almost the same shade of Spanish olive green, not beautiful but very easy to spot in parking lots.

The cops marched, he waddled, and I followed, through a narrow service corridor, past a number of doors marked EMPLOYEES ONLY, the laundry room, and the kitchen, until we emerged at the back of the hotel onto the outside loading dock.

Off to one side was a tall, bearded guy in a stained down jacket. His Big Y shopping cart was crammed with bottles, bags, an American flag, and a padded moving blanket that, like him, had seen better days. Glassy eyes shone out of his dirty face and matted hair; was it drugs, psychosis, or fright?

On the ground, to the homeless guy's right, surrounded by a knot of people, was a muscular body in black jeans and a gray-and-black-striped shirt, legs askew, face covered by an opened and now bloodied copy of yesterday's *Connecticut Post.*

Not far from us two men donned paper jumpsuits and prepared to climb into a giant Dumpster. "Why do we always have to do the wet work?" I heard the younger one mutter. "Because we're the new guys," the other one said.

I followed my escorts down the few sticky steps at the right of the dock to where the body was. From the center of the crowd someone barked, "She the one?" The men stepped aside. Hidden behind a cluster of uniformed cops, plainclothesmen, and hotel security was a slight woman who appeared to be in charge.

"I'm Detective Winters. This you?" she asked, holding up my business card. Not too cute, not too boring, tasteful colors. I recognized it immediately, having agonized over it for weeks. I nodded yes.

"Dirty Business. You wanna explain that?"

"It's a gardening business. Dirt. It's a joke," I said lamely. "Get it?" Obviously the woman had no sense of humor.

"You know this guy?"

I'd seen dead bodies before, and steeled myself for the shock. Winters used two gloved fingers to lift the tented newspaper. She kept her eyes glued to my face as she peeled back the paper and showed me Nick Vigoriti's rugged face, which now had a gaping two-inch hole in the forehead.

I fought the urge to puke . . . then quickly lost the fight, turning and narrowly missing my own bare toes and the dead guy's Italian shoes.

"Whoa, that's what we call contaminating the crime scene." She snickered, stepping aside to avoid any backsplash. I swung around, unsteady on my feet, bumping into Hector and bouncing off his barrel chest. He grabbed me with both hands so I wouldn't fall back onto the body or slip on the remains of my club sandwich.

"What's the problem?" Winters said. "This should be right up your alley. You're in a dirty business and he's taking the big dirt nap."

I was retching again, bent over, hands on knees, and couldn't answer.

"It's a joke," she said. "Get it?"

Two

It was a safe bet that Detective Stacy Winters and I wouldn't be going shopping together anytime soon. After making the cheap joke at my expense, she realized I *had* contaminated her crime scene and, annoyed, she continued to interrogate me without so much as missing a beat or offering me a tissue or a glass of water.

She was about my height, five foot six, but, unlike me, had no hips or breasts to speak of. Her closely cropped hair was bleached white and stuck out in little spikes all around her face, making her look more like an android or the lead singer in an eighties girl band than a cop in small-town Connecticut. She wore a dark blue suit and a plain white shirt, a sexless version of the outfit I'd been wearing a few hours earlier. Clumpy black mascara was her one concession to femininity and against her pale skin and watery blue eyes it made her look faintly psychotic. She shook some Tic Tacs into her hand and popped them into her mouth, but pointedly didn't offer me any, even though I could have used one.

"I don't think it's suicide," she said. "What do you think?" She looked me over, and took her time before saying anything else. I searched for the good cop since she was obviously the bad one.

"You're not Nicky's usual type," she said. "He likes—liked—blondes. And generally a little older, more seasoned, he'd say."

"I don't know what he liked. I just met him tonight. He helped me into my room." That elicited muffled laughs from the group until she ordered them to settle down.

Suddenly, I was conscious of standing, in thin pants and a threadbare top, in the cool night air, in a sea of cops and security guards. I struggled to maintain my dignity and cover my chest, which was threatening to reveal just how cold I was. The homeless guy and I were in this together; he must have found the body. In a show of solidarity I made eye contact with him and folded my arms in an attempt to stay warm but also to hide my shaking, both from the cold and from the experience.

"Nick Vigoriti," Winters recited. "Low-level hood, lucky in love, unlucky in everything else."

I wiped my mouth with the back of my hand, too polite to spit, but desperately wanting to. "If you knew who he was, why did you need to call me?" I asked. She wasn't used to being challenged and, not surprisingly, didn't like it.

" 'Cause you were seen with the deceased," she said, flipping through a small blue notepad, "interviewing him, apparently, a few hours ago." She looked at me as if she'd caught me in a lie.

"I wasn't interviewing him. He just happened to sit down next to me. I'm not sure it's germane to your investigation, but I'm writing an article. On gardening."

She seemed to find that amusing. And under the circumstances, it did sound pretty lame. "Right. And all those other girls at the bar are writing their theses on the sex lives of the Arapaho Indians."

This drew howls from her captive audience of subordinates, who, I had the feeling, knew they'd better laugh at the boss's jokes. It only confirmed my earlier notion that the woman and I didn't have the same sense of humor.

"The article is for the *Springfield Bulletin*. It's on the titan arum in the hotel's lobby." My illustrious press credentials and the Latin name failed to dazzle her. "The common name is the corpse flower—" my voice trailed off.

"This is the only corpse I'm interested in right now," she said, pointing to Vigoriti with her pen. She read me the high points, or low points, of Nick's career from her notepad, but something told me she knew them by heart. Only in his thirties, Nick had been an old-timer at Titans, hanging around the place and running errands since he was fourteen and the hottest action at the hotel was Monday night's mah-jongg and Thursday's amateur night.

"In and out of trouble, in and out of beds," she said, staring at me to see if she'd gotten a reaction, "at least on weekdays when the husbands weren't around." She shared Nick's penchant for stating the obvious.

The way Winters told it made me think she and Nick had some history, but I couldn't tell if it was business or pleasure. Since she hadn't asked me a question, I kept silent. It ticked her off.

"So why'd he have your card? Were you two planning to tiptoe through the tulips together?" Another chuckle from the troops.

"Of course not." I told her about the glass enclosure and how I'd suggested to Nick that I might have a buyer for it.

"Everything's for sale at Titans," she muttered. "Where is Bernie, anyway?" she asked, looking around at her crew. "Didn't I tell someone to drag his sorry butt down here?"

Just then, the loading-dock doors flew open and a big man in a cream-colored suit, with Brillo-pad hair, bleached teeth, and a tan to rival George Hamilton's, powered toward us, arms out to his sides.

Bernie Mishkin took up a lot of psychic space. A big man to begin with, he seemed intent on expanding his territory with sweeping arm gestures and a cloak of cigar smoke that I suspected was permanent, like that *Peanuts* character who was always surrounded by dirt.

"What the . . ." He stared down at Nick's body and bit his left knuckle. His hands flew to his chest operatically, as if he was having a heart attack. "Nicky, Nicky, Nicky." He looked around plaintively. "I'm glad Fran isn't here to see this. She'd be inconsulate. He was like a son to us." The group didn't offer much sympathy, neither did I. I stood there wondering if *inconsulate* was really a word.

"What happened, Stacy, I mean, Detective?"

"Who knows, Bernie? Nick stepped on some toes. Always did. Who knows that better than you? And he had some questionable friends." She switched from comforting to faintly confrontational in a heartbeat and a look passed between them that suggested she thought Mishkin was one of them.

"Anything *you* can tell us?" she asked.

Mishkin could have had a career in overblown amateur theatricals. He threw his hands in the air; if he could have torn out little tufts of hair, I think he would have.

"We weren't close these days." He sighed, finally clasping his hands. "I'll admit it. He . . . we . . . had words."

Winters pulled Mishkin away and continued questioning him about three yards from me. With Mishkin's back to me, I couldn't hear what they were saying. The homeless guy was leaning on his cart and haltingly giving his statement for the second time since I'd arrived. He sipped a clear liquid from a two-liter bottle, and rearranged his bag collection, tucking in a thin black leather strap. I nearly asked him for a swig of water to clean my mouth before coming to my senses.

More interested in Mishkin now, Winters seemed to have forgotten about me; I was left with Hector, the deceased, and the stinky puddle I'd made. After fifteen minutes, which seemed longer given the stench and the chilly night air, I challenged her again. "Are we finished, Stacy, I mean, Detective? Much as I'd like to help you, I don't think there's anything I can add to your investigation since I didn't know the victim," I said. I mustered all of my nerve, refolded my arms tightly across my chest, and tried to look tough. Easy in Doc Martens, not so easy in flip-flops.

"Just when we were getting on so well," she said.

"I'm sorry," Mishkin said, as if noticing me for the first time. "Have we met? Were you a friend of Nicky's?"

"She was seen with the victim a few hours ago," Winters said.

Mishkin stepped toward me and stared, trying to recall if he'd seen me before.

Winters gave me her card and lapsed into cop speak, telling me to call her if I remembered anything else that might have a bearing on the case. *Fat chance I'd get in touch with her again of my own free will.* As soon as Lucy checked in, we were checking out.

A news van arrived and Winters motioned for Hector to get me out of there; I was more than happy to leave. I followed his squat body and knocked knees, retracing our steps back to the loading-dock doors; then I remembered about the greenhouse.

"Mr. Mishkin," I said, turning, "could I possibly have fifteen minutes of your time tomorrow?"

Mishkin looked at me, then Winters, bewildered and almost nervous. "Sure," he said, "call my assistant, Rachel, to set up a time." He seemed to be waiting for an explanation. I let him stew for a few seconds.

"It's about the corpse flower."

Three

Once we were away from the real cops, Hector slowed down and regained some of his swagger. He may have even shot his cuffs.

"You get a lot of police activity here?" I asked, speeding up to walk alongside him so I didn't look like I was being ejected from the premises.

He smirked as if it was no big deal.

"We found another homeless guy by the Dumpster once. Got stupid drunk and curled up in a spot where one of the delivery trucks sat idling the next morning. Died of accidental carbon monoxide poisoning. Big Y comes for the food," he added, smiling. "Rachel, Mrs. Page, doesn't like it, but there's not much she can do about it—she can't stay in the kitchen all day."

It must have finally dawned on Hector that he was escorting a not-bad-looking woman through the hotel lobby, so he took the opportunity to flirt. "No one else comes here for the food. Not spicy enough. If we had a better kitchen, maybe there wouldn't be so much food thrown out," he joked.

He eyed me up and down. "You don't look like a gambler."

"I'm not," I said. "Why do you ask?" I thought of Nick's dumb comment about the odds favoring the house.

Hector told me that most of Titans's guests checked in and then left for the mega-casino twenty miles down the road. At one-third the cost for an overnight stay, Titans was a cheaper alternative for the nickel-slots crowd and the road warriors on limited travel-and-expense accounts who worked the Boston–Hartford–New York corridor.

But they didn't spend much on food and beverages here, and that was where the real markup was.

"Judging by the Maltese and her owner, you're pet lovers, too," I said.

"Yeah, we're pet-friendly. Fran"—he remembered himself—"Mrs. Mishkin loved animals."

So the Mishkins had somehow held on through the lean years with this motley clientele and, according to Hector, had recently, miraculously, been given the promise of an influx of cash from a Chinese investor named Wai Hi. But right now, the Mishkins were hanging on by their fingernails.

As we made our way out of the labyrinth of service corridors, past the much-maligned kitchen and into the all-beige lobby, I envisioned a change in decor to foo dogs and red tasseled lanterns. I wondered aloud why a Chinese businessman would want to invest in a nearly bankrupt hotel in Connecticut.

"Wai Hi made a lot of money in Malaysia. Solid-gold-faucet-kind of money—like that guy who had the six-thousand-dollar shower curtain," Hector said. "He's smart, that Bernie. He's got an in with the foreign press." Which meant that four or five times a year a busload of European journalists stayed at the hotel and went outlet shopping the next day. The idea was that they'd write about the experience when they got home to the Netherlands or Italy or wherever they came from.

"Publicity," Hector said, tapping his temple. "Bernie's always thinking about the big picture. In two or three years, we could have bingo tables all over this room," he added, spreading his chubby arms and fingers out wide, in an unconscious imitation of his hero.

Now, bingo, to me, conjures up very fond memories of Aunt Jo and little plastic disks and bottles of red ink with spongy tips. Warm and fuzzy, but not exactly the stuff that dreams are made of.

"Is bingo such a hot ticket?" I asked stupidly.

"Shows what you know. That's how they all get started," Hector said, as if I were an idiot or a five-year-old. "The big ones. Foxwoods, Mohegan Sun. All the Indians start with bingo."

We walked through the hotel lobby, past the corpse flower, past the sparsely populated bar, and I flashed back to grade school, trying to remember if I'd ever heard of an Indian tribe called the Mishkins.

Hector deposited me at the elevator and I assured him I could make it to the sixth floor under my own steam. Just then, Oksana, the bartender, ran over to us. She was shaking and jabbering in two languages.

"Is it true?" she asked, her accent growing thicker. She folded and refolded a thick wad of cocktail napkins.

Hector nodded.

She looked at me, in my revealing outfit, and must have gotten the wrong idea. She spat out a stream of what might have been Ukrainian and ended with the one word I could understand: "bitch."

"Hey, I didn't do anything. They just found my business card on him." The girl started to whimper again and Hector put his arm around her. Celine Dion's heart was still going on in the background, accompanying Oksana's sobs.

"I'm sorry for your loss," I said. "I know you were friends." I didn't know anything of the kind but she was obviously distressed and I thought that would make her feel better. Instead, her sobbing escalated into wailing and she glared at me, as if Nick's death was somehow my fault. Hector rescued me from the unspoken accusation.

"C'mon, *mamí*," he said to her. "I'll get someone to drive you home."

This is so not what I thought I'd be doing tonight. I thought I'd be hanging out with an old friend, maybe treating myself to a massage, writing my little story. Not to be.

The first time I'd stood in that elevator, four hours earlier, Nick Vigoriti was handsome, sexy, and alive. The thought gave me the chills. Upstairs, I fumbled with the key again, but happily the green light flashed and I was able to unlock the door. As soon as I walked in, I noticed the smell. And it wasn't me. True, I'd just spent the last hour barfing near a Dumpster, in the same vicinity as a cigar-chomping troglodyte, a homeless guy, and a dead body that—to put it bluntly—was no longer sending out pheromones, but *I* wasn't what smelled. An unmistakable odor assailed my senses. Smoke. Not a fire—cigarette smoke.

I called out, thinking it might be the maid, or Lucy, who occasionally lit up despite my threatening to stage an intervention if she continued. No answer. I backed out of the room, gently closed the door, and hurried to the house phone near the elevators to call security.

Within minutes, Hector Ruiz reappeared.

"What's the problem, ma'am?"

I have a thing about being called "ma'am." I'm just not ready for it. Standing there in my hoodie and flip-flops, I didn't think I looked like a "ma'am," either.

"Hector, after all we've been through together, I give you permission to call me Ms. Holliday."

"Yes, ma'am."

"Someone's been in my room."

"Housekeeping has probably been there, unless you had a Do Not Disturb on your door."

"I did, but it's not there anymore. Besides, would she be smoking?"

"No, ma'am, Ms. Holliday. Of course not, but it's possible she had a cigarette on her break and the smoke lingered." Maybe he was right. I thought of the rancid cigar smoke clinging to Bernie Mishkin's hair and clothing. Hector spoke Spanish into his headset and I understood enough to know he was summoning the maid to the room.

"She'll meet us there," he said.

"I hadn't thought of that possibility; I don't want to get her in trouble."

"She won't get in trouble. We'll just clear this up." Hector was all business now, and obviously enjoying his starring role in such an eventful night. It must get boring with nothing to do except strong-arm the occasional drunken suburban suit.

We walked back to my room, arriving at the same time as the maid, who got there so fast she must have been behind one of the staff-only doors on the floor. She was a sleepy coffee-colored woman in a pale gray uniform with white collar and cuffs that reminded me of the little paper frills some people put on their Thanksgiving turkeys. She and Hector had an exchange in Spanish that was way too fast for me to follow. At the end, her eyes welled up with tears, and her neck, behind the ridiculous collar, flushed bright red.

"Look," I said, "it's not that big a deal. It's just that it's a no-smoking room. I'm sensitive."

"She says she was here to turn down the bed about an hour ago—that would have been when we were downstairs—but she doesn't smoke. Let's go in, shall we?"

He opened the door with his passkey and the maid and I followed him into the room sniffing like hounds on the trail. Only I detected anything. Faint, but definitely there.

"I know someone's been in here," I said.

"Do you want to check to see if anything's missing?" Hector asked, unconvinced.

The laptop was still on the coffee table, and my backpack was on the love seat. I checked my wallet; nothing appeared to be missing.

The maid shrugged and said something to Hector in Spanish, then went over to the bed to straighten the dust ruffle.

"She says, Perhaps it was *su esposo,* your husband," Hector translated. I had the feeling he might have left out a few choice words, like *crazy gringa.*

"Well, then we'd have a small problem since I don't have a husband."

"The maid says she saw the two of you going into the room earlier."

What was she talking about? Usually it's the semihysterical woman who claims to have been with someone that no one else has seen—not the other way around.

"Young, dark, macho," Hector prompted. "Perhaps a friend?"

"That guy? That was the dead guy, Nick what's-his-name." Not the smartest thing to say to a man who'd just heard me vehemently deny knowing Nick Vigoriti.

"My key wasn't working. He helped me get into my room. That's all. He didn't come in." Tired of explaining, tired of being interrogated, I said, "You're right. Everything's fine." I sniffed the air and smiled. "There's no cigarette smoke here. All in my head. I'm sure it's just the strain of the evening's events." I couldn't wait for them to leave so I could triple-lock the door, rinse the taste of vomit from my mouth, and plunder the minibar. Now I did want an alcoholic drink. And carbs. Who could blame me for indulging in a little stress eating after a night like this?

The maid was still muttering, mostly to herself. She brushed by us to get to her cart outside and then returned to the bed. She smoothed out the turned-down corner of the duvet and placed a chocolate on each of the pillows.

They left with assurances and apologies—hers sincere, his, I wasn't sure about. As I closed the door, the maid continued her monologue.

"*Pero nunca olvido las dulces,*" she said, shaking her head.

Four

I took a shower, brushed my teeth, then raided the minibar. Pretty much the dictionary definition of doing things ass-backward, but I didn't care. The minibar was almost as empty as my fridge at home. Some high-fat salty snacks sat in a wicker tray on the counter, and inside the minifridge, screw-top wine, beer, and a door full of little nips. I took out a Sam Adams and searched for an opener. None. Probably pinched by the last guest. I rummaged in the black hole of my backpack, spilling my wallet, phone, and the sediment from my bag onto the coffee table, hunting for my Leatherman, but I couldn't find it. Too tired to keep looking, I held the lip of the bottle on the edge of the small refrigerator and slammed the heel of my fist down on the bottle. The top popped off just like it did when I was eighteen. It was nice to know I still had the touch.

I collapsed on the love seat, put my feet on the cheap coffee table, and swigged hard. I found the remote and switched on the television again, wondering if Nick's death had already made the local news. I clicked the channel-up button until I found a station running the story. There was Mishkin tearfully bloviating to a bubbleheaded reporter, so I cranked up the volume. Then the voiceover continued. "Persons of interest are being questioned in this deadly encounter that has all the earmarks of a drug deal gone terribly wrong," and then the video cut to *me* being led through the lobby by Hector! I leaped to my feet, yelling at the screen, "Person of interest? I know what that means."

I didn't know which bothered me more, that some incompetent reporter had wrongly referred to me as a "person of interest" or that I thought I looked dumpy in my low-slung yoga pants. I considered calling Winters to complain but knew she'd only lay the blame on the press, so I didn't waste my breath. This "person of interest" would be out of town tomorrow and it couldn't come fast enough for me.

I grabbed a pack of Oreos from the minibar and tore the package open with my teeth. *That's right, take it out on your own hips.*

I tossed the package aside and flopped back down on the love seat, shoveling my belongings back into my backpack.

That's when I noticed that underneath its leather cover my phone's message light was flashing. Not voice mail; another text message from Lucy. *Two men.* What the hell did that mean? *Two men are better than one? Two men are better than one girlfriend?* Was she coming or not?

I stared at the message and read it again. Something about it was off. For one thing, Lucy generally signed with the letter *L* or *Loo-scious,* if she had the time. It wasn't like her to blow me off completely without more of an explanation—unless a job or a man was involved. And with Lucy, each was a distinct possibility.

Lucy and I had met in high school, back in Brooklyn, when we unwittingly shared a boyfriend. Lars was a beautiful Danish exchange student with cornsilk hair and Mick Jagger lips. She had him Tuesdays, Thursdays, and Saturdays, and I had him Mondays, Wednesdays, and Fridays. Presumably he rested on Sunday, but we were never sure—there were a dozen sniffling girls at his going-away party. You could either get angry or laugh it off. We laughed it off and got close.

We were in and out of each other's lives during college, then reconnected a few years back at a television programming market in the south of France. Not bad for two Brooklyn girls. We were about the same size and had the same long dark hair, but hers was more likely to be sporting hand-painted caramel highlights and a four-hundred-dollar haircut and mine was more likely to be stuffed up under a Knicks hat, especially now that I'd made the move to the hinterlands and couldn't afford a chichi stylist, even if one had existed in Springfield.

I texted her back, saying I'd call in the morning. If I hadn't committed to writing the article for the *Bulletin,* I would have been packed and on the road back to my nice little house, where there were no dead bodies, or at least none recently. I'd give the corpse flower overnight to show some more signs of life, but after my chat with Mishkin I was out of there. Maybe I'd give Hector a nice tip and ask him to send me a picture.

Revived by the beer and annoyed by Lucy's e-mail, I brushed away the crap on the coffee table and turned on my computer to work on the story. I did an online search for anything I could find on the titan arum and the Titans Hotel. I sent them to my desktop at home, where I'd print them out in a day or two when I sat down to finish the piece. Then, just because I had the time and a second Sam Adams, I did a search on Indian casinos.

Hector was right, it had all started with bingo. In 1972, the state of Connecticut enacted something called Las Vegas Nights, a limited measure to help churches and nonprofits raise funds. Good people at the Knights of Columbus or Elks clubs, raising money for team uniforms, the way I imagined it. That was the intention. At the time no one could have guessed how dramatically that statute would change Connecticut's future.

Fifteen years later, when the United States Supreme Court ruled that state and local governments couldn't regulate bingo parlors on Indian reservations, those two events combined to open the door for the mega-casinos that have since appeared, Oz-like, on the Connecticut landscape—not always with the blessing of the neighboring towns, and not always benefiting the people the ruling was passed to help.

And now, even though the Las Vegas Nights statute has been repealed, any group of people claiming Native American heritage can seek federal recognition and announce plans to open a casino. Some residents were against them, but plenty of others were more than happy to bankroll the legal fees for their claims in the hopes that the tribe would eventually be recognized and they'd share in the multibillion-dollar-a-year business Connecticut casinos have become.

I sent the casino info to my home computer along with the rest, got up to stretch, and walked to the minibar for another beer. I leaned across the bed to pluck a foil-wrapped chocolate from the pillow on the far side. One of *las dulces*, the sweets. What had the maid said? Something about forgetting the sweets? But *nunca*, what did that mean? I'd have to ask Anna when I got home.

Before I knew it I was out cold.

Some time later the phone rang. It was Rachel Page, Bernie Mishkin's assistant. He'd been called away to a meeting in Hartford but could see me at 6:00 P.M. when he returned. I peeked at the digital clock on the nighttable, 7:13 A.M. Why the hell was she calling so early?

Rachel sounded surprised when I answered, but offered me a late checkout and a free spa day if I wanted to stick around to wait for Mishkin. She sold me on the idea of a body treatment—after my Dumpster experience, it sounded like a good idea, although nothing less than sandblasting would make me feel clean again.

"Sveta is wonderful. You'll feel like a snake shedding your old skin," she said.

I mumbled yes and hung up. Why not? Wasn't that one of the reasons why I came . . . a little R & R?

I rolled out of bed and instinctively reached for my phone. One new text message: *Not coming. Lucy*

Five

I left a message on Lucy's cell. It was still too early to call her office, and it would be hours until my appointment with Bernie Mishkin or my spa treatment with the scary-sounding Sveta, so, laptop and camera in hand, I once again set out to explore the hotel.

The Titans dining room had the look of a hospital cafeteria, a little less antiseptic, but not much. It was nearly empty. Based on what Hector had told me, I figured most of Titans's guests decamped for the casino as soon as they woke up to get in a full day of hot slots and video poker—but for all I knew everyone else had heard about Nick and I was one of the few foolhardy guests still registered.

I picked up a newspaper and headed for the deepest corner of the dining room, away from the all-you-can-eat buffet. As late as the murder occurred it hadn't made that day's front page and probably wouldn't until the following morning.

A busty waitress named Laurie came to take my order—coffee, fruit salad, and whole wheat toast.

"You can get the buffet for two dollars more," she said mechanically, before the words had fully left my lips. I resisted the temptation.

While I waited for breakfast I logged on to the computer and within minutes I was in Sumatra, Indonesia, the only place in the world where the corpse flower grows in the wild.

Anyone in the United States can buy a titan arum bulb from a mail-order catalog. Still, it's appropriate that the bestselling plant in America is called the impatiens, nature's answer to the artificial flower. Most people don't have the patience to babysit spring bulbs planted in the fall, much less one that takes seven years or longer to bloom—if it ever does. Flowering is exceptionally rare for corpse flowers in cultivation, and it only happens when the plant is hand-pollinated—the botanical equivalent of in vitro fertilization.

I scrolled through the listings of documented flowerings from the last ten years: the Brooklyn Botanic Garden, Virginia Tech, the University of Wisconsin at Madison, the Royal Botanic Gardens at Kew. It was hard to imagine Bernie Mishkin's hotel joining that rarefied group, even temporarily.

My order came fast and I slid the laptop over to the left-hand side of the table so I could pick at my food and continue reading; the waitress sneaked a peek as she refilled my coffee.

"Is that what that thing in the lobby is gonna look like?" she asked, pointing to the screen with the coffeepot. I held my breath, visualizing scalding hot decaf soaking in between the keys of my new Dell.

"If we're lucky," I said, nudging the computer a few inches farther away.

"They've had someone out there measuring it every couple of hours for the last two weeks. Damn, that's like me weighing myself when I'm on a diet—every couple of hours, to see if *not* eating that cookie has made me any thinner." I could identify with that; it made me like her.

"I'm not surprised about the frequent measurings," I said. "It can shoot up as much as five inches in a day. When the growth slows down, that's when you know it's ready to flower."

"You ever seen one?" she asked, ignoring the couple who had just walked in. She waved her hand in a motion that told them to seat themselves.

"Once. A few years ago in Brooklyn."

"Brooklyn, Connecticut?"

It's a fact that most people from Brooklyn, New York, think there's only one Brooklyn. When you can see chewing gum in France with a picture of the Brooklyn Bridge on the package, and T-shirts in Zanzibar with the Brooklyn Dodgers logo on them, it's a natural assumption, but it's not true. At least four states have Brooklyns and Connecticut was one of them.

"New York."

"Oh."

I might as well have said Mars.

"You know," she said, leaning in and getting close again with the coffeepot, "from this angle it looks a little like . . ."

"Yup."

She let out a whoop and moved off to the newcomers' table, a big grin on her face as if she finally got the joke.

I tried to use my found time well. I'd ratcheted down quite a bit since my BlackBerry-24/7 days but still found it difficult to sit still for long stretches of time. And single-tasking made me feel like a shirker.

I e-mailed Caroline Sturgis and rescheduled for early the next morning. Then I left Sumatra and went back to work on Caroline's garden design and crossed my fingers that she'd sign off on the plans. Now that Laurie and I had shared diet tips and a naughty joke, she kept me refueled with coffee as if I was a hotel regular. I asked her if she liked working there.

"Oh, yeah, beats unemployment." Laurie had worked at Titans for eight years, since her youngest started school. Her husband had worked in a local factory that had closed so he now had a two-hour commute each way. "That's why I take the early shift. Otherwise I'd never see him."

She liked Bernie more than Rachel but thought that was natural, "him being a man and easier to deal with."

"I guess she's gotta come off that way," Laurie said. "She's one of those hard women. Hard to deal with, hard to like."

Bernie was the opposite. A pushover.

"Those Ukrainian girls walk all over him." A slim blonde in a rabbit-fur jacket caught her eye and sat at the counter. "I gotta go. That's a pal."

By the time I packed up my computer to leave, they were breaking down the breakfast bar and setting up for lunch. Similar to a cruise ship, life at the Titans Hotel revolved around mealtimes. I felt guilty for not generating a bigger tab so I left Laurie a generous tip and headed for the lobby, looking for something else to occupy my time until my spa visit this afternoon.

"Thanks, honey," Laurie yelled after me, pocketing the bill. "See ya tomorrow." Not likely.

I made my way to the corpse flower, waiting for whoever it was that had the task of monitoring the plant. I didn't have long to wait.

She bounced in, wearing a UConn baby T-shirt and a canvas cap I would have described as early Mao, but college kids probably called something else. About nineteen years old, she was a sturdy girl with pale freckles and light brown hair in a thick, no-nonsense ponytail, set high on the back of her head. Her rectangular-framed glasses gave her an edgier look than her unmade-up, corn-fed features did, and I guessed that was the intention. She said her name was Amanda.

After I introduced myself as a fellow gardener, Amanda Bornhurst invited me into the greenhouse to watch her work. According to Amanda, when the Mishkins had agreed to buy the six-year-old corpse flower, they hadn't had the slightest idea it would need daily attention and the aforementioned hand-pollination, if it was ever to flower.

"How did you get the job?" I asked.

"Mr. Mishkin called the plant clinic at the arboretum. They turned him on to my school's extension university. My professor offered me the assignment for extra credit. I've never spoken to Mr. Mishkin personally, but I send him e-mails of my progress reports. He's very into it."

Amanda's gear was in a canvas bag, with skinny pockets and loops for tools. She set it down on the small table next to the wrought-iron bench where I was sitting. She took out her records, notes, and tape measure and laid them out with the precision of a surgical nurse.

"He's the only one, though. No one else seems to care much about it," she said, shaking her head and causing her ponytail to swish back and forth rhythmically. "Wait till it flowers, though. It's practically a miracle."

She explained how she'd cut a thick wedge out of the bulb to collect the pollen and used a paintbrush attached to a wire hanger to deposit it on the stamens. Then she slid the chunk of plant material back into place. Now it was close to flowering.

"Okay, drumroll." Amanda stood on a small ladder. In a practiced move she hooked one end of a metal builder's tape measure under one of the ladder's feet. "Ninety-seven and a half inches. That's only one and a half inches more than yesterday. We're getting close!" She was as excited as if this was her personal space launch or the countdown to midnight on New Year's Eve. I snapped her picture as she climbed down from her perch.

"So what does that mean?" I asked, although I sort of knew.

"As long as it keeps growing, it won't bloom. The aroma is really starting to kick in. It's intense from up here. Wanna smell?"

I passed; it was pretty pungent from where I sat.

She'd never seen one in the flesh, so to speak, but the Internet was filled with pictures. It would be impressive. "We've got a few more days," she said. "Then pow!" She may have had a few more days, I didn't.

The girl entered her observations in a Huskies notebook and took pictures of her own. I checked my watch. Still hours until Bernie Mishkin returned. If this baby wasn't going to bloom today, I'd be on the road shortly after I saw him. But I did have a story to write.

I offered Amanda fifty bucks for copies of her digital pictures, gave her two of my cards and asked her to write her e-mail address on the back of one of them.

"I'll send you the pictures, but I don't think I should take any money," she said, writing down her info. "That might not be right." I was charmed that she was grappling with an ethical issue, so few kids these days seemed to, but I came down to earth when she asked her next question.

"Will I be in the newspaper?" she asked, brightening. I guess the news articles and surveys were true—more young people wanted to be famous than be rich, or successful, although all three would be nice.

"The world-famous *Springfield Bulletin*."

"Cool. Can I get tearsheets?" Tearsheets? Jeez, did she have a publicist?

"Sure," I said. She told me her boyfriend also worked at the hotel and I promised I'd try to mention him in the article, too.

Amanda stashed the ladder behind the bench, ushered me out of the greenhouse, and locked the door with a heavy chain and a bicycle lock.

"It's nothing personal," she said, "just security." I laughed to myself and decided not to tell her that while the hotel was securing a glorified houseplant, a guy had been killed there the night before.

"No probs."

Amanda bounded out of the lobby, to field hockey practice or some other overbooked suburban kid activity, checking off another item on her busy schedule.

It was still thirty minutes until spa time. I moseyed around the lobby, trying to eat some clock when I saw Oksana setting up the bar and chatting with a guy who punctuated his speech with frequent wheezing. The previous night she'd all but accused me of being involved in Nick's death so I slipped outside to the pool area, staying under her radar by using that ability to make myself invisible that I'd cultivated in high school. I knew high school was good for something.

Six

If the Titans spa had ever been an ongoing concern, it must have been back in the days when women in turbans stood in exercise machines and tried to jiggle the fat away. A glass door on the second floor was labeled Gaia's Palace—at least someone knew their Greek mythology. The room held little more than a bare reception desk, some candles, and a small bamboo plant in a shallow dish of wet pebbles—dollar-store nods to an Asian sensibility, but they were trying.

While I waited for someone to greet me, I poked around, eventually sneaking a peek at the spa's appointment book. I was curious to see if there were any other clients that afternoon, or if I was the only one who'd been coerced into using the spa. Just as I opened the book, the door to the treatment room swung open, and I slammed the book shut.

No waiflike creatures in black here. No long-necked model wannabes moonlighting from their jobs as haughty hostesses in trendy restaurants. Just Sveta. Quite possibly moonlighting from her other job as a professional wrestler. She led me into the treatment room that she had already prepared and I followed her in with all the enthusiasm of someone about to be strip-searched at the airport.

"Salon receptionist is off today," she mumbled in a heavy Russian accent. "We have big group coming soon, so she will be here long hours." I thought Sveta was lying, but gave her credit for being a good employee attempting to keep up appearances for the guests. "Today we have salt scrub."

Apparently I didn't have a choice. I was here. The salt was here. And so was Sveta. She ordered me to strip down and held up a sheet to shield her eyes while I did. A plastic shower cap and a paper thong were on the table behind me and I put them on as she instructed. New Age harp music played in the background. Relaxing was difficult. Finally I hopped on the table and lay facedown while she covered my butt and legs with a cool cotton sheet.

Wearing scratchy white gloves, she began exfoliating my back, starting at my shoulders and moving her hands in short downward strokes.

"First we do this. Slough off dry skin from winter. Should have humidifier. Heating and air-conditioning is bad for skin."

She finished my back and repositioned the sheet to expose a different part of my anatomy. I was just about to drift off.

"You are writing about flower?" she asked.

Was it in the company newsletter? I told her I was.

"Is good for hotel?"

I told her hordes of people would visit Titans because of the article. They'd come from all over.

"That's what they say about the foreign writers, but it never happens. And they're lousy tippers."

I could tell that annoyed Sveta because she was scraping at my flesh a little harder than before. That last stroke was almost a smack.

"Terrible thing happened last night," she said, after a few minutes. Was this supposed to be relaxing? Sveta's xenophobia and the police blotter? I grumbled a noncommittal assent. "Bad for hotel," she said.

And not so great for Nick, either.

"He was pretty man, but not to be trusted," she said.

Any thoughts I'd had of a relaxing or therapeutic spa treatment were gone. Now that I was practically naked and under the woman's catcher's-mitt hands, what did she want from me? Could I run out of here in a shower cap and paper underwear if I had to?

I turned my head to the other side to give myself time to think.

"You're right," I said, stalling for time.

She attacked my legs and arms with renewed vigor, brushing so hard that not only would my skin be smooth after this treatment, I might even weigh less. She was really getting into her work now, holding up my left arm by the wrist and sanding me down with a spa glove. Out of the corner of my eye I could see little flakes of winter skin sloughing off.

"He let Oksana believe he cared, but he was a fake." I hoped she didn't have too much invested in Oksana's being jilted, or I'd have no skin left.

"Lovely girl," I said, mumbling into a towel and hoping to diffuse some of her agitation.

"She is, but she's a child. And he was a liar. Nick bought her a few dinners. That was it. She wants to be rescued. You must rescue yourself."

After delivering that insight into her personal philosophy, Sveta finished with my *B* side and I turned over. Why was she telling me this? Was this her own message or one she was delivering for someone else?

"Still," I said, trying to lighten things up, "if all the liars in the world were killed, there wouldn't be many of us left."

Her message delivered, she laughed, deflated my "A" side, then drizzled a gritty almond-scented oil on my skin and worked her hands in small rhythmic circles to distribute the scrub.

When the scrub was finished, Sveta pointed me toward the Swedish shower, where I was pelted by three columns of icy water. I covered my face and let myself be spun around until Sveta took pity on me and turned the water off. She enveloped me in a wall of terry cloth and I shook the water from my eyes.

"When I worked at The Baths," she said, "we would have done platza next, but no oak leaves here."

I'd heard of platza—a friend of mine swore by it. But I hadn't yet warmed up to the idea of paying a stranger to beat me with branches. "Do you mean The Baths in New York City?" I asked.

She nodded. "I lived in Brighton Beach and took D train to the Village. Too expensive," she said, leading me back to the treatment room. "I come back here, more friends."

She patted the table, now covered with a mylar sheet and a thick padded fabric. I hopped on and she proceeded to anoint me one last time. This was the part that always made me feel like a baked potato. She folded the fabric over me and crimped the edges of the mylar so that I was encased in silver foil from my neck to my toes. All that was missing was a sprig of parsley and a dab of butter.

"Twenty minutes. You want washcloth for forehead?"

I passed on the washcloth, but asked her to turn off the cheesy harp music.

"Is no problem."

She killed the music and the lights. Just as she was leaving the room, I saw the lights of the reception area and the silhouette of her next client, a tall man who drew a deep breath and wheezed before addressing Sveta in Russian.

I'd be smooth as a baby's bottom for my meeting with Bernie, but I wouldn't be relaxed until I was vertical, dressed, and out of there.

Seven

Rachel Page looked like a lot of women I'd known in New York—curly chocolate-brown hair, long, like a Portuguese water dog's, overinflated lips, and the semi-Asian look that came from one too many *procedures*. After cooling my heels for twenty minutes in his waiting room, I was finally admitted into Bernie Mishkin's office. Rachel led me to the inner sanctum, pointed me toward a tufted, faux leather wing chair, and quietly left, backing out of the room and closing the door behind her.

One wall was filled with sepia and black-and-white pictures of the hotel during its construction. And autographed head shots of celebrities who'd stayed there in the forties and fifties. I walked around the room, seeing who I recognized.

Mishkin breezed in through a second door to the right of his enormous desk. "Celeste Holm was my favorite. A beautiful woman. And nice. Always treated the staff well. That's how you can tell who's got class."

I sat down and he automatically offered me a drink. I declined, citing my long drive home after our meeting; he poured himself a tall tumbler of something brown.

"Rachel takes good care of me," he said, pointing the bottle toward the outer office. "My sister."

That explained it; I'd had him pegged for the curvy, Hooters-type assistant who couldn't use the computer, couldn't write a letter, but could sharpen his pencil pretty good.

"She's been looking after me for the last few months, since Fran died. All my life really, ever since we were kids in Brooklyn."

"Brooklyn, Connecticut?" I asked.

"There's only one Brooklyn." To Mishkin, there was.

It had been a long time since anyone had asked me where I went to high school, and even though he had twenty-five years on me, we spent a few minutes going over old Brooklyn landmarks.

He looked the same as he had the previous evening, yards of light-colored fabric wrapped around his substantial frame in what had to be a custom-made suit, a white-on-white shirt, ivory silk tie, with a gold tie tack, and a pocket hanky origamied into four perfect points. To his credit he wasn't wearing a pinkie ring.

I was anxious to get on the road, so I got out my pad and launched into some of the questions I'd jotted down earlier that afternoon after my session with Sveta. The staff had been tipped off that I was a FOB, a friend of Bernie's, and plied me with snacks and drinks all day, so I'd sat bundled up by the fifties-style pool guzzling complimentary virgin Marys and making notes.

Mishkin took his time answering, giving me generic answers, telling me to ask Rachel, and repeatedly steering the conversation back to Nick Vigoriti and the *tragic loss of such a fine young man.*

"As I said, I really didn't know him. We just had a brief conversation at the bar." Why was Mishkin grilling *me*? Wasn't I the one who was supposed to be interviewing him?

"I understand why you might not have wanted to say anything last night." Had Hector told him the maid had seen us together? "I've known Nick all his life, and he could never resist a pretty woman," he said, laying it on.

I'm sanguine about my looks. Sometimes I look good and other times, when I'm stressed or tired, I look like the Olsen twins' less normal older sister—bad hair and wild eyes. Bernie leaned in conspiratorially, waiting for me to spill some nonexistent beans. I didn't have any beans.

"So, were you the driving force behind getting the corpse flower for the hotel?" I continued.

"It was Fran's idea." Now I felt guilty for pressing the issue. Fran Mishkin had read an article about the titan arum and had thought it would be a good gimmick for the hotel. She had also suggested an exhibit some years back in honor of their neighbors on the reservation. Bernie called it, an "In-jun exhibit."

"They didn't understand publicity like she did. She was a real marketing genius. We would have gone under years ago if it hadn't been for my Franny." His eyes went glassy, either from the loss of his wife or from the amber liquid he'd just gunned.

"This probably isn't a good idea. I'm sorry to have brought back bad memories."

"My memories of Fran are good. It's just all so fresh. She's only been gone a few months. And now Nicky . . ." The bluster was gone and Mishkin was left staring at his ice cubes. I mumbled my thanks and got up to leave.

"Please, Ms. Holliday. Sit down. I'm sorry. Nicky's death has hit us all so hard." He looked at me for confirmation.

Not me, I thought. *I hardly knew the guy.* And if Mishkin was so broken up about it why did he keep bringing it up? I was tired of denying I knew the guy, so I decided to play along.

"Well, Nick *was* an extremely attractive man." I looked down at my folded hands, feigning grief, to see what Mishkin would do.

"See, I knew you two were up to something," he said, wagging his index finger. His eyes twinkled and he smacked his lips, his bonhomie returning. He poured himself another generous drink, and again tilted the bottle in my direction. Again I passed.

"It all happened so fast," I said, alluding to our totally fictitious yet torrid relationship. I struggled to remember some detail about Nick, or something he'd said to me, to keep the ruse going. "He did tell me that you two hadn't spoken for a while."

Mishkin's smile froze. He drained his glass and made little patterns in the condensation. "Did he say why?" he asked, doing a rotten job of sounding casual.

Ka-ching. I'd touched a nerve. "No. But I know he was sorry about that. I think he was hoping for a reconciliation or a resolution." It wasn't a total lie. Nick did say he'd talk to the Mishkins for me, but it was about the greenhouse, not whatever it was that had caused a dark shadow to pass across Bernie Mishkin's wide face. So was all of Mishkin's hand wringing and hair tearing a fake?

With eerily perfect timing, his sister buzzed him as I chewed over the uncomfortable possibility that Bernie Mishkin was not only not grieving for the dear departed Nick, but that he also knew more than he was telling either me or the charming Detective Winters about Nick's death.

"Sorry," he said, holding a button down on the phone. "International call, London, can't be helped." He nodded periodically but said little. Over the phone, I heard someone yelling.

If Mishkin was implicated in Nick's death, I didn't want to know about it. That was a matter for Stacy Winters, and the other cops, not me. He motioned for me to wait, but I took the opportunity to escape.

Back in my room I threw my things in my bag, still wondering what the hell that meeting was all about. Wasn't it after midnight in London? And I'd forgotten to ask about the damn greenhouse. I called his office as soon as I remembered, but Rachel said he was gone for the day.

"That was fast," I said. "Is there any way I can reach him?"

She didn't respond. This was one closemouthed family. Unlike my own vocal, trusting crew. If someone had called my mother and asked where I was, she'd probably give him directions, whether she knew him or not. *This nice man called. He didn't say what he wanted. Yes, dear, he did say something about being an escaped convict.*

I checked for messages one last time and left two for Lucy, one on her cell and one at her office. The recorded message still claimed Lucy would be in central Connecticut for the weekend. That was odd. Unlike me, who records one outgoing message and doesn't record another until I get a new machine, Lucy changed hers with neurotic frequency, every time she took a trip, and sometimes just for fun. Either this was one hell of a tryst or she'd been called out of town for an even bigger story. That was also possible, given her job, and it was the option I was starting to root for.

One last call before I hit the road—I dialed my pal at the *Springfield Bulletin* to report on the corpse flower's progress, or lack thereof.

"Jon, how's it going? Listen, I don't think this baby is going to pop for another two or three days. Do you really want me to stay up here that long? It's only seventy miles, I can always drive back when it does bloom." I told him what I had and he agreed there was enough pre-bloom material for a Sunday feature, so I closed down my computer while we were still on the phone.

"Guess what? Some guy was killed here last night. I talked to him before it happened."

"Well, it'd be damn hard to talk to him after. You're yakking to me about a potted plant when there's been a mysterious death at the old hotel," Jon said. "You will never be a newspaperman. Spill." Jon must have seen too many old Rosalind Russell movies when he was young and impressionable, and liked to affect a 1940s newshound's lingo. It was quite endearing. I told him as much as I knew.

"What does Lucy think?" he asked. "She's got a nose for news."

"She's not here. She stood me up."

Jon and Lucy had met a few months back, and he nursed a puppy-dog crush on her, which she wisely ignored. He knew about the accident on 95 and offered to contact the local hospitals to make sure she wasn't laid up somewhere. Part of me thought he was overreacting, but in the back of my mind I felt like a lousy friend for not having thought of that; I was too busy working her love life into the equation.

"Good idea. My cell signal goes in and out on the Merritt," I said, "but call me if you hear anything. I'm coming home."

Eight

I'd wasted most of the day waiting for Mishkin, but it wasn't a total loss. Apart from my free session with Sveta, Mishkin had instructed the front desk to comp my stay. Since Lucy and her corporate credit card had never showed up, my friends at the *Bulletin* would be happy about that.

I went outside and waited for the parking attendent to bring my car. Two young guys, one in a gold vest and another exuding all the health and charm of a heroin addict, stood there lighting up. I tried to stand where the secondhand smoke wouldn't drift my way.

The valet pulled my Jeep around to the front of the hotel. I handed him a couple of bucks and pulled out, fiddling with my cell and hands-free cable. I hated talking while I drove, but if Jon or Lucy called, I wanted to know as soon as possible.

There'd be congestion near the hotel, but the Merritt Parkway should be clear by the time I got on it and with any luck I'd be home by 10 P.M.

Can a road be sexy? If it can, then the Merritt is one sexy road. There's a pitch and sway to it that can make you feel like you're dancing with two tons of steel. The more times you drive it, the better you know when to stay to the right and when to lean to the left. And the trees are beautiful. You'd never think that most of the time you're only five minutes away from a Home Depot or a Wal-Mart. There's even a spot near one of the few gas stations where a cell tower has been camouflaged with fake branches—*Pinus cell-ostrobus,* someone had dubbed it—to make it less offensive.

I was about an hour into the drive and the light was fading. Through the trees the sky had turned pink, then orange, then inky blue. The Jeep's headlights turned on automatically. And so did those of the car trailing a little too close behind me. I checked the speedometer. I was going sixty-five mph, fine for me at this hour, and if he wanted to pass, why the hell didn't he just do it? No one else was around. All right, be cool. Some drivers like to have a lead pony, especially at night. I sped up a tiny bit. He kept pace.

A friend of mine used to be a regional sales rep for a pharmaceutical company and found herself driving all over the East Coast at odd hours of the day or night. She bought an inflatable man doll, and would strap him into the passenger seat for nervous-making occasions just like this. She'd put sunglasses and a hat on him, and throw one rubber arm over the back of his seat to make it seem like she wasn't alone. When she started calling him Ronald, we all got a little worried.

Just pass, you moron. I tensed up, then relaxed a bit as we swung around a long curve and I saw a third car behind the guy trailing me.

I knew there was a Mobil station ahead on the right, and decided to stop for a pee break and a diet Snapple, and to lose my convoy.

I signaled well in advance of the stop and pulled in to the middle of the rest area, beyond the pumps, the dog run, and the mini-market.

First one car, then the other, pulled in. They killed their lights fast, and crawled to the far end of the rest area.

Nine

No one got out of either car. And no interior lights suggested that the drivers were either looking at maps or making phone calls. I repositioned my side-view mirror to get a better look at what they were doing. Nada. Were they together? Had they stopped because of me? Why would I even think that? I wasn't usually the jittery type.

I grabbed my bag and casually, *I thought,* jogged toward the presumed safety of the service station's market. So casually I forgot to lock the car. I fished around in my pocket, found the keys, and locked it with the remote, accidentally hitting the panic button that's supposed to keep robbers away, but really only scares the car's owner. No one even reacted. So much for panic buttons.

At the gas pumps, a young woman was finishing up. She looked about Amanda's age, with multiple piercings in the ears, but not in the eyebrows or nose as far as I could see.

The girl tore off her credit-card receipt, then stuck her head in the driver's-side window and poked her sleeping passenger. "You owe me twenty bucks for your share of the gas." The friend mumbled something and twisted herself into an even more contorted position than before. "Missy can sleep anywhere," the girl said to me, when she saw me looking.

"It's a gift."

She finger-combed her long thick hair straight back from her forehead and it flopped right back into the same position, framing her face when she dropped her hand. "You know how far Greenwich is? We're driving to Missy's parents'."

They looked like Greenwich. Blond, blue-eyed, good kids really, but at that stage of life where they could go either way. The piercings could move from her ears to her tongue or further south, and the artfully streaked hair could turn to a modified Boy George with splashes of green or pink if my last visit to the East Village was any indication of current trends.

Missy and her friend were only half an hour away, and I was twenty minutes from Springfield, but I took my time giving her directions, chatting and keeping one eye on the two cars at the end of the lot. What the hell were they doing? Or didn't I want to know? And when did I get so nosy? I'd heard there were rest stops on the highway that were unofficial hookup spots but had never really believed it. And if that's what they were up to, what was it to me?

The girls finally drove off, and I entered the minimarket, setting off the shrill buzzing doormat, startling me and rousing the small dark clerk who was catching some zzz's behind his Plexiglas shield. His goldtone name badge read RAVI.

He nodded at me, as much to wake himself up as to suggest anything remotely like customer service might be forthcoming. Then he pointed to the back of the narrow building, where the restrooms were, before I'd even asked. I still had a funny feeling about those two cars outside. I was in no hurry to sequester myself in a small locked room, so I killed some time reading the nutritional information on a package of Ring Dings, then started mindlessly plucking items off the shelves as if I did all my grocery shopping at the gas station: water, diet Red Bull—the nice jumbo cans—nuts . . . I drew the line at Slim Jims, even though there'd been a time in my life when I'd considered them one of the basic food groups, along with beer, muffin tops, and martinis.

When I was reasonably sure I was just being 'noid and the drivers outside were merely having a snooze, a squeeze, or a snort, I headed for the ladies' room. I grabbed a handful of my shirt and used it to keep from actually touching the doorknob. Not bad. Pretty clean actually, but that didn't stop me from meticulously layering the seat with toilet paper before sitting down. I know, it's neurotic, but the lessons of youth are never quite forgotten—I had a friend who always traveled with her own over-the-door hook so she'd never have to put her handbag on the floor of a public bathroom. Undoubtedly something her mother once taught her.

I'd just unzipped and dropped trou when through the opened window I heard a car start to pull out and then stop after only a minute. I heard a door slam. Moments later the doormat's jarring buzzer sounded. Trapped in a toilet, I could be in big trouble. I sat there paralyzed. What could I use as a weapon if I needed one? A plunger? A toilet brush? Only if I touched them and that was a big if since whatever was outside was probably less deadly than either of those germ-riddled items. I was staring at the bathroom's small shuttered window, trying to picture my hips squeezing through, when I realized I was being ridiculous—the victim of an overactive imagination. I zipped up, washed up, and threw some cold water on my face, patting dry with a rough paper towel. This time, I wrapped another towel around the doorknob to let myself out. The door opened into the bathroom and I held it ajar with my butt and turned to watch the balled-up wad of paper bank shot into the trash.

"Nice shot."

I spun around in the tiny bathroom, slamming my shoulder into the door and my hip into the doorknob and coming face-to-face with the large pockmarked nose of a man with no visible neck. His double and triple chins melded into his shoulders and chest and I imagined that naked he must look something like the Michelin Man. Not a pretty picture.

"Thanks," I mumbled. I tried to get past him and we did that little dance you do when two people are trying to be polite and accidentally keep blocking each other's way, only this didn't feel accidental or polite.

"Sorry," I said. "I'll just scoot by." I skipped around him fast, my fingers grazing the cold leather of his jacket, which was so voluminous it must have cost two cows their lives. I was ready to make my exit when Ravi, the clerk, called to me.

"Lady, lady, I am ringing your order."

Michelin Man flashed an oily grin and positioned himself right behind me, between me and the door. I gave him a weak smile and moved closer to the counter to put as much distance between us as possible. He didn't seem to be buying anything; he just stood there, his frankfurter fingers laced in a loose cat's cradle, his stubby thumbs tapping together to some internal melody.

"If you're just getting cigarettes or something, you can go before me," I said, "I have a lot of stuff."

"I don't smoke. Filthy habit." He shrugged and showed me three candy bars buried in his laced fingers. "Sweet tooth." I was stuck.

Inside my pocket, I separated my keys so that there was one in between each finger of my right hand. That way if I had to throw a punch, it would do more damage. I'd read that in a women's magazine somewhere and hoped it was true.

"The big bottle of water is on sale, wouldn't you like that one instead?" Ravi asked.

"Sure, why not?" I said, watching him leave his perch to get the water. Every item was rotated twice, to find the bar code. It was an excruciatingly slow process.

"When you spend over twenty dollars, you get a free lotto ticket," he said, finishing up the sale. "Would you like to pick some numbers?"

Here I was, trying to get the hell out of there, and this guy was bucking for employee of the month.

"It's okay, I'm not much of a gambler and I'm in a bit of a hurry."

"Are you sure?"

"Positive," I snapped, taking out my wallet and clumsily nudging out my credit card with my left thumb.

Ravi flipped the card over. "Please, miss, you haven't signed your card."

"There's a picture of me on the front of the card, what else do you need?" I was instantly sorry for being rude.

"Not much of a gambler?" Michelin Man said. "That's too bad. I, myself, am a big believer in luck." I hoped he didn't think he was going to get lucky with me. What was with these guys? Was I sending out horny, lonely signals? First Nick, then Bernie, and now this manatee.

I couldn't manage a signature with my left hand, so I reluctantly let go of my keys to finish the transaction.

"Thank you very much, Miss Holliday," Ravi said, handing me my receipt.

Excellent. Now the Michelin Man knew my name. Luckily it was a fairly common one. If he was a crazed stalker, there'd be three or four other victims named Holliday before he got down to the *P*s in the phone book. Surely the cops would find him before he got to me.

He still hadn't moved, and now I was grateful that the clerk was taking so long, double-bagging my purchases for the mad dash to my car. I redid the key arrangement in my pocket and planted my feet in case I had to land a punch and make a run for it.

Just then, the cavalry arrived. We heard them first. It sounded as if a helicopter was landing outside, then the sputtering died down. The doormat shrieked again and five guys who could have been the defensive line for the Hell's Angels' football team came in. The Michelin Man's face dropped; so did poor Ravi's. I was the only one grinning like a happy idiot.

One guy camped out in the doorway oblivious to the fact that standing there kept the doormat buzzer going. The other four scoped out the dining options. The biggest walked over to the shelves near the coffee machine. He picked up a cellophane-wrapped Danish and dropped it as if it was radioactive.

"Hey, man. I can't eat this crap. This stuff'll kill you."

Ravi looked hurt. "I have the PowerBars," he offered weakly.

"I know a great diner!" I said, a little too loudly. "I do." I quieted down and tried to sound seductive instead of like a basket case. What the hell, three other guys thought I looked hot that day, even if they didn't have the most discriminating taste. "It's only ten minutes from here," I lied. "My girlfriend owns it. I'll take you." I flirted with the big one closest to my nemesis, who looked a lot less threatening now.

That was how I got my Harley escort out of the service station, away from the Michelin Man, and all the way to Babe's Paradise Diner.

Ten

I was channeling Cher and mumbling the words to "Believe" under my breath. Five beefy guys on four bikes followed me to my car. Whatever it was the Michelin Man had in mind, he was no match for my new best friends, and we left him and Ravi, and whoever was in that second car, scratching their heads in the service station minimarket.

Charlie seemed to be the big dog. The biggest physically, he had the biggest bike, two-thirds as wide as the Jeep and encrusted with pipes and grilles that did who-the-hell-knew-what but made the bike look like a small spaceship. He stayed on my left, tossing me the occasional smile or thumbs-up, and the others trailed us, playing leapfrog until we got to the diner.

By the time we'd pulled into the Paradise parking lot, I'd convinced myself that Charlie and his friends had saved me from worse than death, and as they dismounted, I gave them bear hugs

and back slaps as if we'd just ridden cross-country together instead of twenty minutes on a tree-lined suburban road.

"Party of two . . . three . . . *six?*" Babe asked, as we tumbled
into the near-empty diner. Charlie's arm was still around my
shoulders. "Any more coming?" She craned her neck to look into
the parking lot.

Wanda "Babe" Chinnery owned the Paradise. Although she is
one, I hesitate to call her a retired rocker because she still rocks,
she just doesn't do it onstage anymore alongside a metal band and
in front of thousands of screaming kids. She waved the guys over
to the corner booth in the back and pointed to some menus
stacked by the window.

"How old is that decaf?" I asked, joining her at the counter.

"Not that old," she said, pouring me a cup. "You know, I'm the
last to throw stones, but when I said you should get out more," she
whispered, "this wasn't exactly what I had in mind." Babe had been
playing matchmaker for me for the last year, with zero results, so
she was surprised to see me come to the diner with five guys in tow.

"So who are your friends, and why are you sitting over here?
This isn't some weird initiation rite, is it?"

"I couldn't decide between them. I brought them all here so
you could help me choose." She squinted at the unlikely assort-
ment of suitors. For a minute I think she believed me.

"I'm joking. They got me out of a sticky situation on the Merritt," I said.

"Did they?"

I told her what had happened, or nearly happened, at the gas
station.

"So you thought two guys were following you and decided it
was better to have five guys following you? That makes sense."

Put that way, I wondered if I'd made a huge mistake and whether tomorrow's *Bulletin* headline would read "Local Businesswoman and Customer Found Raped and Murdered."

I looked back at my escorts. Charlie was well over six feet tall, with one earring, no weird insignia on his leathers. I wasn't up on my bandanna symbolism but his was black and partly covered thick snowy hair. He smiled at us through his close-cropped beard and revealed a puckish gap between his front teeth. Santa, or his evil twin? The others were all permutations of the same guy . . . a little thinner, a little taller, two mustaches, one soul patch. They all wore black leather chaps, like hundreds of helmetless bikers you can find on the Merritt any day of the week, but especially on Sundays, when they all seemed to converge on Norwalk, just south of the service station where I'd met these guys.

"Safety in numbers?" I wondered aloud. The bikers called Babe over.

Watching Babe walk, when she's working it, is a thing of beauty. I can only imagine what she was like twenty years ago, shaking her tambourine and just about everything else for the Jimmy Collins Band. They'd traveled all over the United States and Europe and Babe had the stories and the scars to prove it.

She wore sleeveless tops twelve months out of the year to show off her well-defined arms and sported a collection of tats that would have impressed an NBA player. Her black apron was tied low and tight around her narrow hips, and she employed her no-fail *Yeah, I'm sexy, and I know where to kick you if you mess with me* walk. It had its usual intended effect. Two were in love, two were in lust, all were in awe. Including me.

She took their orders and I tried not to stare. Instead I sucked up my coffee and absentmindedly gazed out the window, looking for the two clowns we'd left at the service station and profoundly happy they were nowhere in sight.

The Paradise was across the road from a typical suburban retail strip—liquor store, karate school, nail salon, Dunkin' Donuts—and somewhat less typically a police substation. A few years back these outposts were common in suburban Connecticut and may have even helped keep the petty crime rate down, but budget cuts and benign neglect had forced many of the substations to close, and the rest, like this one, to be virtually abandoned for most of the day. A faint light shone from behind the blinds, but there were no other signs of life.

Babe came back and handed the bikers' orders to Pete, the diner's cook. There was always a chance that a cigarette ash might make its way into the food, but that aside, dining at the Paradise had gotten a whole lot better since Pete discovered the Food Network, and the captivating trio of Sara, Rachael, and Giada. Pete routinely threatened to leave this Babe to go chop vegetables for one of those babes, but smart money says he won't.

"Grilled chicken Caesar, two spinach salads, and two turkey clubs, I think we're okay," Babe whispered to me.

I'd heard of people being able to predict criminal behavior by computing a person's gender, age, youthful exposure to violence, even head shape, but never by what they ordered in a diner. I wanted to believe she was right but what did she expect them to order—Twinkies with chocolate sauce? But, Babe wasn't finished. She had more anecdotal evidence.

"And furthermore," she said, "they're riding Harleys. It's the rice-burners you have to watch out for. They ride for speed not comfort. I prefer a man who doesn't go too fast." According to Babe, men on Japanese bikes were nine times out of ten more likely to be thugs than men riding Harleys. I don't know where she got her statistics but since I had zero information on the subject, I believed her.

My biker friends considered dessert, but decided against it after a lengthy debate on how much further they'd ride that night, and whether or not the sugar overload of one of Pete's four-story desserts would cause them to crash, nutritionally speaking. Despite Babe's confidence in her culinary assessment of my escorts, I wasn't comfortable leaving her alone with them so I stuck around after finishing my coffee.

"You boys have a good ride?" Babe asked.

"Coming back from Marcus Dairy. Just went for the day," one of them said.

Marcus Dairy was actually a working dairy but better known as a hangout for bikers all over the East Coast. One of the guys had had a breakdown and had to leave his bike there for a couple of days. As Charlie and the boys left, they promised to stop in again on their return trip. From the way Charlie was looking at Babe, it was a sure thing.

"I don't think I've ever been here this late," I said, helping Babe pull the shades down. She opened the register, counted out some cash, and put it in a zippered bank bag. She put a hundred dollars back in the drawer and left it open. "So the robbers don't feel like they've wasted their time and trash the place."

"Are you ever nervous," I asked, "all by yourself?" I followed Babe out and she yanked the front door shut.

"I don't scare easy. Besides . . ." She seemed on the verge of telling me something, then pulled back. "It doesn't happen that often. I close when I feel like it, and Neil usually picks me up after work. He's just away for a few weeks. His mother's sick."

"That's a drag."

Neil MacLeod was Babe's . . . what? Hookup? Lover? Boyfriend?

Can you have a *boyfriend* after the age of thirty? Whatever she called him, he was handsome, young, Scottish, and visiting home, where his parents owned a small pub and inn in Cardhu, on the Malt Whisky Trail.

"Is it serious?" I asked.

"Don't know. But it was time he went back. He hasn't been home for ten years. Listen, if you're planning to meet up with those guys, go for Charlie," she said, putting the receipt tape in her bag. "That gap between the teeth presents possibilities," she added, always looking on the bright side.

"Please. They served a purpose and are now, conveniently, out of the picture."

Babe climbed into her car and I climbed into mine. How long had it been since *I'd* been home? And where was home anyway? New York City, where all my friends were? Brooklyn, where my eighty-five-year-old aunt still lived in the house where she and my father were born? Boca Raton, where my mother inexplicably moved after my father died? Or was it finally Springfield? The small house and big garden that the bank and I owned, but only I lived in?

In A.D. 93, the Roman poet Horace wrote: *This is what I prayed for! A piece of land not so very large, with a garden, and near the house a spring of ever-flowing water, and up above these a bit of woodland.* That's exactly what I had. And that's where I was going.

Eleven

I hauled myself up the stairs, dumped my things in the living room, and dropped the mail on the kitchen table. Despite the decaf, I was wired. Maybe I shouldn't have cleaned out the mailbox at the foot of the driveway. It was mostly junk anyway—catalogs, campaign literature, and flyers from cleaning services and house painters. I always wondered if they targeted *my* house. *Good grief, that hovel needs a coat of paint.*

My house is the most modest in the neighborhood. Wetlands restrictions and the nearby bird sanctuary saved my little bungalow from spec contractors who'd cock it up with fake dormers and stone facing and then try to flip it to some middle manager who'd sweat the mortgage until he thought he could palm it off on someone else. I told myself the neighbors silently thanked me for maintaining the character of the place, but couldn't be sure since I didn't know any of the neighbors, so I never had the opportunity to ask.

On my left was a formerly noisy guy who'd either grown up,

gotten married, or died; I hadn't seen or heard him all winter. That's the way it was in the suburbs if you had no PTA or country-club connections. You could be almost as anonymous as you were in a big city.

I trashed the solicitations and the mailings from grinning office seekers with jackets not so casually thrown over their shoulders. Problem was, I couldn't toss the bills. Dirty Business was doing okay, but I was still getting used to the challenge of being flush for half the year and rolling change the other half. I wasn't eating cat food, but it had been a long time since I'd treated myself to a splurge. That was the real reason for my trip to Titans. But that plan had backfired when Lucy didn't show and a dead guy did instead.

I checked my cell messages again. Nothing from Lucy. I wasn't worried about her, just curious. And maybe a little jealous. I hadn't been in a relationship for over a year, and if anyone had asked I would have said that was okay, I had my hands full running a business. But I hadn't had an adventure for even longer—and I was due.

There was just one call from Anna, my sometime assistant. I left Lucy another message, then checked my home phone just to make sure she hadn't tried to reach me on that number. Zip.

It was midnight. Fatigue was setting in; bills were staring me in the face. I thought of opening them, but . . . *Screw it, they'd be here tomorrow.* The article for the *Bulletin* would bring in a few bucks, and more important, maybe a client or two. Hector and Bernie were right about that, publicity was key. And first thing in the morning I'd call on Caroline Sturgis, my rich suburban matron.

I meant to wake up at six and get a run in before driving to Caroline's. Instead, I slept in until after eight when I heard a key in the front door and Anna Jurado sang out my name, "Meez Poh-lah!"

March through October is garden season in my part of Connecticut. For those eight months the newlywed team of Anna and Hugo Jurado worked for Dirty Business. I couldn't afford to pay them the rest of the year, and they generally returned to Mexico anyway, but for those months we were a real company, not just a woman with stationery and business cards who still felt a little like a fake. Hugo was a master in the garden and helped me hire temporary workers when I was lucky enough to need them. Anna made appointments and kept the books.

I ran my fingers through my hair, pulled on a sweatshirt over my pajamas, and went into the kitchen to greet Anna. She was resplendent in a tomato-red track suit with white jeweled stripes down the sides puckering and threatening to give in to fabric fatigue.

"*¿Qué tal?*" I asked, starting to make coffee.

"I am very well, thank you very much. And how are you today?" Anna and I played this little game practicing our language skills on each other. If we'd been keeping score, she'd have been killing me.

She and Hugo were married less than a year ago in a ceremony that made the local paper, not because they were members of Springfield's elite, but because they, and I, had been players in the biggest news story to hit the town since the hurricane of 1938.

I willed the coffeemaker to speed up. My appointment with Caroline was for nine o'clock and I had a twenty-minute drive to the Sturgis home. I didn't want to be late. Anna saw me eyeing the clock and shooed me out of the kitchen.

"Get dressed. And fix your hair. I will bring you the coffee when it's ready."

It says something about my current grooming habits when the cleaning lady is giving me beauty tips. I hadn't totally gone to seed. I still worked out religiously—that part hadn't changed since my move from New York—but I had to admit my hair was getting a little shaggy. It was just easier to pull it into a ponytail and put on a baseball hat. And like most gardeners I had perennially grubby hands.

I took a quick shower and pulled on jeans, a boy's thermal T-shirt, and the hoodie I wore the previous night. Back in the kitchen I twisted my wet hair into a knot and fastened it with a big clip. Then I took a fistful of bangs and distributed them evenly across my forehead.

"That's a very attractive look," Anna said, handing me a mug. "You look like you are going to deliver newspapers on your bicycle."

"*Gracias.*"

It was the kind of crack I expected from a woman in full war paint and rhinestones at breakfast. And Anna wore her plus size regally; where I neurotically counted every calorie that passed my lips, Anna happily indulged in whatever culinary delicacy struck her fancy, with no shameful morning-after guilt, no slavish adherence to slimming black. *More to love,* she'd say. I was trying hard to adopt her philosophy.

"Kids don't do that anymore," I said, shaking some cereal into my coffee, "deliver newspapers. Nowadays, they have Internet consulting gigs. I met a ten-year-old last week who had classier business cards than I do. Ivory laid stock—looked like Crane's, for crying out loud. She was leaving a stack of them at the Paradise Diner in a little metal holder near the real estate booklets. Eerie." I poured more coffee over my cereal.

"That's disgusting. You should eat something more substantial than that."

"I'm multitasking." I spooned the concoction into my mouth. "I had a big breakfast yesterday; I have to be in Greenwich by nine," I said, checking my watch. I took a last spoonful of cereal, grabbed my backpack, and bolted down the stairs. "I'm outta here."

"Are you going to see Mrs. Sturgis? Make sure you get one-third upfront," she said as I flew out the door. Always looking out for me. "*Usted nunca . . .*" she started to yell, "you never remember."

I'd try. But Caroline Sturgis was one of those women who didn't think much about money because apparently she'd always had it. She always paid, but she always paid late. Last year Anna had suggested we start charging her one percent interest; we did, and she still paid late. Bills were minor annoyances to her.

Caroline lived one town over, where the house numbers were harder to see because the front doors were so far from the road, and the mailman could listen to an entire pop song in between deliveries because the mailboxes were that far apart.

The Sturgis home had been designed by a student of Frank Lloyd Wright—poor guy, he was probably ninety years old and still referred to as a student. Caroline's place was magnificent—lots of levels, built-ins, and fireplaces—and all natural materials: stone, wood, and slate.

The long, wooded driveway led to the side of her house and the deck, which faced a private pond. To the right of the house was a small garden and a shallow reflecting pool. Beyond that were Caroline's tennis court and a large barn renovated to serve as a guesthouse. On the fringes of the property was the town's arboretum.

It cried out for Prairie or Asian garden themes, but Caroline wouldn't hear of it, preferring annuals and a cottage look more suitable to a New England saltbox. It killed me. And if the "student" was still alive it'd probably kill him, too.

Last year she'd let me test one perennial grass in a container near her tennis court, so I had my fingers crossed I'd get to push the envelope again this year and go beyond mere petunias and alyssum. It could be a notable addition to my résumé, the way the Peacock house had been last year.

I pulled into the Sturgises' driveway through two stone pillars topped by Mission-style light fixtures. Following the drive around to the left, I continued about a hundred yards to a separate three-car garage. As I was getting out, the garage door opened; the driver was just as startled as I was. He leaned out of the car, with a stunned expression on his face, and backed out a little too fast, kicking up pea gravel and spinning his tires. He put the car into drive and pulled out, crushing some snowdrops at the side of the driveway.

Inside, Caroline heard the tires squeal and came to the screen door to see what was up.

"Hi, Paula," she said, shielding her eyes and watching as the car pulled onto the road. "I don't know why he has to drive like that. He can't be late; he's been reading the paper for the last forty minutes. C'mon inside."

He was Grant Sturgis, Caroline's husband. I just caught a glimpse of him, but he looked slightly familiar. Caroline thought we might have met at the opening ceremony for a garden I restored, but with his bland features and sandy hair, Grant could be mistaken for almost any slight, not unattractive, thirty- to forty-year-old man. Generic, both-hands-in-their-pockets guys who could be found in every restaurant, mall, and private club in the country.

Caroline, on the other hand, had a spark. True, it was currently hidden under a velvet headband, and the safe suburban armor of flats, slacks, cotton shirt, and sweater tied around her neck, but it was there. And in danger of combusting, if she kept feeding it alcohol.

I'd met her two years ago. She was dropping off and I was

furnishing my new house at the Springfield Historical Society's Thrift Shop. We shared a few laughs over some of the merchandise— long, skinny prints of big-eyed children, crafts projects gone horribly wrong. We also shared a fondness for the two older women who worked there, known affectionately as the Doublemint twins because time and friendship had turned them into carbon copies of each other.

When Caroline found out I had a garden business she squealed that I was just the person she was looking for, although I had a feeling she was lonely, and anyone that day would have fit the bill. We went back to her place and after a brief discussion of the colors she liked we had a handshake deal. I would plant a thousand spring bulbs all around her tennis court. It wasn't my idea of a beautiful design but clients were hard to come by, especially in September, so I said yes. Each year I encouraged her to be more adventurous.

My entire house could have fit in Caroline's kitchen, and on the spotless marble countertop was a pitcher that experience had told me was filled with mimosas. Strong ones.

As the client, Caroline Sturgis could get as highly smashed as she wanted to at nine in the morning. Good sense and something my doctor had said to me at my last checkup about "high liver enzyme levels" kept me on the straight and narrow. A big part of my last job had been social networking and that had inevitably involved a certain amount of drinking, but those days were over, especially now that I had a mortgage and two employees counting on me to make payroll. And I couldn't afford to be fuzzy-headed if there were power tools around.

Caroline poured herself a tall one and me the same despite the fact that I'd waved my hand over the heavy-bottomed tumbler she'd set out. I moved the glass to one side and set up my laptop to bring up the garden rooms I'd envisioned for her property. The screen quickly filled with pictures of small shrub and perennial beds I thought would work for the various spots in her garden. She pretended to pay attention but I could see her mind was elsewhere. Right then it was on her drink, which she downed as if it was straight orange juice.

"Caroline, is this a bad time? I can come back later."

I didn't really want to, but I needed her full attention or else she'd revert to impatiens and petunia mode, instead of even considering the more substantial changes I was proposing.

"No, no. Don't go. This is as good a time as any. You've done all this work and here I am daydreaming."

If it was a daydream, it wasn't a pleasant one. Caroline's normally smooth forehead was as wrinkled as a Klingon's and there were two deep grooves in the shape of the number eleven at the top of her nose.

She let me drone on about ornamental grass, Russian sage, and rudbeckia, but she was lost in thought and it wasn't from weighing the benefits of miscanthus versus fountain grass. I worried about mixing business with personal stuff but decided to ask her what was the matter.

"I just feel so useless these days," she said. "Molly's away at school and Jason will be leaving in January. And Grant's been traveling so much lately. He just got back from a week in Boston, and now he's off to Chicago for four days. I guess that means his business is doing well but I thought we'd have more time together now that the children were older, not less."

When it came to relationship advice my specialty was "Screw him. He doesn't deserve you." That worked pretty well for most of my single New York friends. Here in the 'burbs I was in uncharted territory. I didn't have the first clue as to how to comfort an empty nester.

"I take a few classes . . ." she said, trailing off. "Mostly to get out of the house and see people."

My laptop went into sleep mode; I pushed it back a few inches. I was antsy to get back to work but it was pointless until Caroline finished unburdening herself.

"What kinds of classes are you taking?" I asked. Part of me really cared.

"What haven't I taken?" She threw her head back, laughing and rolling her eyes. "Real housewife stuff. You'll think they're silly. I guess they are."

"No I won't. Tell me."

"This year, glassblowing and wreath making. I drive to the city for the glassblowing class and take wreath making at Mary Ellen's Craft Shop in New Canaan."

"They're not silly; my mother does a lot of that stuff." She winced. Wrong move—what woman wants to be compared to her friend's mother? I regrouped. "That's impressive. I'm not good with my hands except for digging. So what have you made?"

"Nothing. That's just it," she said, recovering from the insult and pouring herself another drink. "I lose interest. I have a room filled with half-finished projects—shell art, calligraphy, pottery. That hobby room is a shrine to my failures."

"You shouldn't think of it that way. At least you've tried." I took a sip of the mimosa, just to be sociable. There was dead silence for a minute. Trying to empathize, I told her about the tag-sale treadmill in the garage that silently mocked me every time I pulled out of my driveway. "And who doesn't have an unfinished scarf or poncho in her closet?" I said. "Although if you're talking about baby booties from fifteen years ago, you might want to pitch them."

She finally cracked a smile. "I can't seem to throw any of it out. The potter's wheel I bought after I saw the movie *Ghost* for the twelfth time. The loom I searched all over the Internet for. I was so happy when the box finally arrived, and I made exactly one ugly potholder with it."

"Have a tag sale or take them to the thrift shop. The twins would be thrilled to have them. And dumb schmucks like me will be happy to assume the burden of ownership until they realize they aren't going to use them either. Maybe there's really only one potter's wheel and one loom," I said, "like they used to say there was only one fruitcake that was passed around and regifted during the holidays."

Caroline was laughing and sniffling now, finishing one drink and instantly pouring herself another. She made a move to refill my glass then realized she didn't need to.

She'd snapped out of her funk, but drinking at this rate, what was she going to be like by noon? If she wanted to drink herself stupid by lunchtime that was her call; it wasn't up to me to give her advice, but that didn't stop me. I repositioned my laptop and slightly, unnecessarily, moved her glass just out of her reach.

"You're a big girl, Caroline, you know what you're doing. But maybe you're focusing on keeping your hands busy when you should be thinking about keeping your mind busy." Which she couldn't do if she was plastered.

She stared blankly into space.

"Forget it. I don't know what I'm talking about," I added quickly, fearing I'd overstepped the bounds of our quasi-friendship. "I'm just trying to be solutional. That's my nature."

"No. You're right. That's it," Caroline said, the light dawning. She raised her glass to toast me, and I obliged by taking another small sip from mine. "So what do you think I should do?" she asked, reminding me of the eager interns we'd had at my old company.

"Well, first you need to decide what you want in your garden."

The lines on her forehead disappeared as if they had been Photoshopped out. She reached for drink number four, but didn't take a sip, and I could tell Caroline was busy plotting some activity other than merely saying yes or no to my designs for her property. She nodded absentmindedly at almost everything I suggested and I began to wonder if she was really agreeing or was just wasted.

A scratching sound came from another room.

"What's that?" I asked.

"Oh, that's my houseguest," Caroline answered, sliding off her high-backed kitchen stool. She crossed the kitchen floor on unsteady, ballet-slippered feet to open a narrow door that led to her mudroom. Out popped a small white dog.

"There you are, precious. Did you miss your Auntie Caroline? Paula, this is my new friend, April." A small white Maltese that looked very much like the one I'd seen at Titans two days earlier in the care of a full-figured redhead.

Twelve

What were the odds? You could go to any park or dog run in Connecticut and yell Maggie and a dozen pooches would come running. And there was no shortage of Tesses, Maxes, or Rileys. But April was not a common name for a dog in these parts. It was like naming a dog Barry or Helen. It just wasn't done that often.

Caroline told me she was doing a favor for a colleague of Grant's who'd had to unexpectedly join him on a business trip and hadn't had time to find a pet sitter.

"Grant brought her home last night. To keep me company, I guess. Isn't she darling?" Caroline bent down to give the dog a scratch and a gourmet dog biscuit she fished out of a decorative tin on the counter.

You'd have to have some cojones to fly off on a tryst with your girlfriend and make your wife watch the woman's dog. From what I'd heard about him, Grant Sturgis was too much of a wuss for that brazen a move. Still, who knew? I was hardly an expert on suburban mores. Or men.

Grant Sturgis was a management consultant, whatever that meant. Everyone I knew who was unemployed refers to himself or herself as a consultant, but apparently there are people who really do it, and full-time, not just while they're waiting for the permanent job to come along.

According to Caroline, who'd quietly gone back to sipping her mimosa, Grant's work took him from Chicago to Georgia to Massachusetts, with the occasional trip to Europe. Despite her halfhearted attempts to join him, she never went. Every time she'd brought it up, he'd mumble something about boring clients, lengthy business dinners, and generic hotels. With that kind of review, I'd have stayed home, too.

"It can't be that boring," she said. "Chicago has museums, Marshall Field's, Buddy Guy's." Shopping on the Miracle Mile and Frango mints, yes, but I hadn't pegged her for a blues fan.

"Marshall Field's isn't there anymore," I said. "And B. B. King's is a lot closer than Buddy Guy's."

"You're right," she said. "It's not him." Had I said that? Maybe I was better at this suburban advice thing than I realized.

"I need to find something more mentally engaging," she announced, nuzzling the tiny dog she now held with both hands.

I steered her back to our garden discussion. Seeing the dog had put some very uncharitable thoughts about Grant Sturgis in my head—I didn't like the idea that he might be boffing some cocktail waitress while making his wife pick up his mistress's dog's poop. I longed for the old days when my pals had easier problems like "It's Thursday, why hasn't he called?"

Under the circumstances, I felt a little guilty but got Caroline to sign off on plans and purchases for the garden; I should remember to get all my clients tanked before meetings. I watched the wrinkled forehead return along with a determined little set to her mouth.

As I got up to leave, she mumbled something about going out, too, so when she wasn't looking, I reached into the tin that held the dog biscuits, got one for April, and left Caroline's car keys in the tin. Not to drive her crazy, just to keep her in the house long enough to realize driving was a bad idea.

The three spoonfuls of cereal I'd had for breakfast were starting to feel lonely in my stomach, so I turned left out of Caroline's driveway and headed back to Springfield for an early lunch at the Paradise.

I pulled in past a line of vehicles that made the diner's parking lot look like an emissions control station on the highway. As always, whatever the hour, size, or temperament of the crowd, Babe had everything under control. I spied one empty stool at the far end of the counter and elbowed my way through a sea of wide-bodied truckers whose haunches were spilling over the edges of the diner's counter stools. It reminded me not to order whatever they were eating.

Business had picked up since Pete started his television cooking lessons and Babe now had three sullen waitresses helping her out at lunchtime instead of just one. Paulette, Theresa, and Alba were busy so Babe motioned for me to help myself to a cup of coffee and a newspaper until things died down a bit. I slipped behind the counter and served myself.

"How goes it?" she asked, when the crowd had thinned.

"It goes. Looks like your business is booming."

"It's Pete's fault. When he was a lousy cook, I had more time to read; now my TBR stack is yea high." She held a hand up to her hips. "And back then I didn't have to play den mother. Look at those three. They're worthless as waitresses, but the little one

has a pretty good voice. The one with the black hair plays bass."
Having spent some of the best years of her life with a band, Babe
still had a soft spot for rock and rollers. And although she denied
it, I think she enjoyed playing den mother.

"Where'd you find them?"

"They came in late one night," she whispered, "after an open
mike night at Boomer's. They were pretty upset—it didn't go so
well. I told them if they worked the lunch shift, four days a
week, I'd give them stage pointers plus salary and tips. We'll see
how long they last. Are you eating or is this one of your liquid
lunches?"

"Eating. I'm ravenous." I ordered a turkey and sundried tomato
wrap, something Pete had recently added to the menu courtesy of
Giada De Laurentiis.

Babe stuck the order slip into a revolving rack behind her and
spun it around like a prayer wheel, then brought me more coffee.

Two cops from the substation across the road came in, and
Babe left me to say hello and seat them. Just then, something in
my backpack rumbled and I recognized the sound as that of a new
text message. I expected it to be Lucy, but it was Caroline Sturgis.
*Thanks for listening and for moving my keys, Sneaky Pete! You're a good
friend. Call me tomorrow, I have a great idea!*

I didn't need a 9 A.M. drinking buddy, and Caroline's last great
idea had involved thousands of bulbs the size of cocktail onions.
Was I a good friend? I didn't bestow the *F* word easily. I generally
thought of people as acquaintances until years had passed and
they'd lost most of their fur like the Velveteen Rabbit. But maybe
that was another New York habit I'd soon be jettisoning. If we
were friends, should I have said something about April and the
tacky woman I thought was her owner? I wondered how Caroline
and the pooch were getting along.

I nursed my food until most of the lunchtime crowd had departed and Babe had time to sit and catch up.

"Okay," she said, hauling herself onto a bar stool on her side of the counter, "what's on your mind?"

"What makes you think there's something on my mind?"

"C'mon, you haven't camped out here this long since the early days when you had two clients and one of them was dead."

I left names out of it, and she leaned in so none of the stragglers would hear. "What would you do if you thought the husband of a friend was having an affair?"

"Easy," she said, straightening up, disappointed that my problem wasn't more challenging. "Do nothing. Say nothing." She made a zipping motion across her lips.

"Really?"

"Absolutely. First of all, it sounds like you don't really know, and second of all, there's nothing in it, either for you or your friend, for you to be the one who drops the bomb."

It wasn't the answer I was hoping for.

"Look, if you're wrong, you'll be persona non grata. If you're right and they split up, you'll be the unwelcome reminder of her humiliation. If you're right and they stay together, you're the friend that knows too much. And if one of them kills the other, then you'll have to testify."

She had a point.

Thirteen

My afternoon schedule was full, too full to hang out in the local diner gossiping about my neighbors. In the same way that
everyone in Connecticut wants their pool opened on Memorial
Day weekend, they all want their garden service started at the
same time. I didn't have many clients with great swathes of lawn
to maintain, with all the attendant chemicals to apply. Caroline's
lawn was the largest, and I'd let Hugo handle that, unless the big
idea she'd talked about was turning it into a meadow. But that
wasn't likely.

There were three nurseries to visit to reopen accounts and
place orders. I spread my business around so all the dealers would
know me, and each supplier had its own strong suit—shrubs,
perennials, trees. Besides, if I was ever strapped for cash I'd have
good credit at all three.

Before heading to the first nursery, I stopped at Lowe's. One of
my other clients had a stand of sedge that had been planted by the

previous owners and ignored for years. The grasslike plant was now threatening to take over her driveway. My plan was to divide it and plant clumps in containers dotted around her property; it would be a nice tie-in with the rest of the landscape, and not expensive.

I could have used a saw but after nearly taking off my left index finger once with a chain saw, I stayed away from most power tools and all but the smallest folding pruning saws. Dueling pitchforks were my weapons of choice. If I plunged each of them into the center of a plant, face out, I could push the forks apart— or step on the backs of the tines—to divide the sedge, or any other overgrown grass or perennial.

This would be the first of many garden-season trips to a big-box home center. For the most part, only amateurs or the truly desperate braved the throng of afternoon do-it-your-selfers who required a full lesson with the purchase of every item, but my schedule had changed and I had no choice. I made a beeline for the garden section, just coming to life with flats of herbs, pansies, and early spring annuals. I blew by the plants, grabbed two pitch-forks, and after a quick credit-card swipe I was on my way.

The nursery was bustling. Forklifts moved mountains of bags of mulch, which made the place smell like a redwood forest. The help was happy to see me. Small-timers like me signaled the return of the busy season. And I was the perfect customer, knowl-edgeable, not big enough to take away serious business from them, and, on a good day, cuter than most of the sweaty, big-bellied guys who had open accounts with them. And thanks to Anna, I paid my bills on time.

Damn, I'd forgotten to get the partial payment from Caroline. Anna, my chief financial officer, would be unhappy. Whatever. I'd make a note to ask Caroline for it next time we met. I loaded up on plant material, arranged for larger shrubs to be delivered, and headed for nursery number two. It was after six P.M. by the time I got home.

I knew something was different the minute I pulled in: some of the stones I'd used to border a bed at the foot of the driveway had been driven into the ground. The old UPS deliveryman had done a number on it on a few occasions. After I complained the new guy was very careful—one of those men who prided himself on his K-turns and parallel-parking abilities. But I didn't see any packages in front of the garage, where he'd have left them, so I inched the car up the driveway, looking for signs that anything else was amiss.

At the top, I got out of the car, leaving the driver's-side door open. A few steps to my right I noticed that a stone trough filled with sedum was crooked. For some reason, I reached into the backseat and retrieved one of the pitchforks I'd just bought, and walked to my front door. As if the out-of-place planter wasn't telling enough, the door was unlocked and partially open.

Pitchfork in hand, I tiptoed up the steps to the front door and yelled for Anna. No answer. I yelled again. Using the fork, I nudged the door open and peered inside. The place had been trashed.

I dropped the pitchfork, ran back to my car, and tore out of the driveway, plowing over stones and ground cover and driving them farther into the garden beds. I didn't stop until I was near the diner, but instead of turning right into Babe's, I made a sharp, screeching left into the strip mall opposite the diner and pulled in right in front of the Springfield police substation. The surprise turn pissed off the driver behind me, uncorking his bottled-up road rage. He let out a stream of anatomically impossible suggestions, but I didn't care, I was too busy controlling my breathing. I rested my head on the steering wheel and exhaled heavily. Hands shaking, I turned off the engine and got out of the car.

Most small retail strips in Connecticut, and probably everywhere in the United States, look the same—overgrown dollhouses or model-train layouts, with a central pitch or cupola. Painted in pastel colors with white trim, the miniature towns look as if Santa's helpers should be inside the shops hammering away at toys. This one was no different.

I took the stairs two at a time and banged on the door of the police substation with my fist. Nothing. I bent over and squinted through the bottom of the miniblinds, where I thought I saw a faint light.

"Hey, anybody in there?" I yelled, banging harder and rattling the glass in the door.

Two people from the nearby Dunkin' Donuts came out and stared on their way back to their cars. A father put his arm around his little girl as if to protect her from the crazy lady. I sat on the steps of the Hansel and Gretel–like structure and dialed 911, telling the dispatcher what had happened and that the cops could find me across the road at the Paradise Diner.

Fifteen minutes later, Sergeant Mike O'Malley and a police cadet who didn't look old enough to be an Eagle Scout met me at Babe's. O'Malley and I didn't exactly go way back but we'd gotten chummy since a garden restoration last year had me up to my elbows in dirt, some of it criminal.

He slid into the booth opposite me; the rookie stood. Babe brought O'Malley a coffee and squeezed my shoulder. "You two play nice," she said.

"This used to be a quiet town until the rough element from New York moved in," he said, taking the toothpick out of his mouth.

That was my cue that O'Malley and I were back in our wisecracking-but-I-really-like-you stage, which seemed to precede the who-the-hell-do-you-think-you-are stage, followed by a repeat of stage one. It was a game I was getting used to, and each time we played it, we revealed a little bit more of ourselves. We haven't approached the *F* word yet, but we were moving in that direction.

"I take that as a compliment," I said.

O'Malley wasn't technically handsome, but he had that teddy-bear thing going. Some women like that. I happen to be one of them. He was very fair, with dark hair, pale blue eyes, and just enough padding to keep things warm on a cold spring night.

Not that I knew it from personal experience. There'd been something brewing under the surface when we first met, but when he was hot, I was cold, and vice versa, so nothing ever happened and we'd settled into a platonic relationship.

In the wintertime, people tend to stay put in Connecticut, at least I did. I stayed home, worked out, read, and planned my gardens for the big thaw in March. I don't know what O'Malley did, but now that the weather was warming up the locals were showing themselves again, like crocuses or carpenter ants.

Some people would have hated that enforced hibernation, but I'd spent the first thirty-three years of my life in a big city and now nothing represented luxury to me more than the sound of . . . silence. No horns honking, no cell phones, and none of their suburban counterparts—lawn mowers and leaf blowers.

O'Malley told me a police cruiser had been close to my house when my 911 call was received, so someone had already been there. No sign of the perpetrator, but I was right: the house had been ransacked.

"That much *I* could tell. Did you boys have to go to cop school to figure that out?"

The rookie's eyes widened.

"Ms. Holliday's our resident pain-in-the-ass. She did a little detecting about a year ago and now she thinks she's on the job."

O'Malley chugged his coffee and stood up to leave. "Are you ready to go back to the scene of the crime?" He rode with me in the Jeep and we followed the kid in the patrol car.

"Recruiting them kind of young, aren't you?" I asked.

"New program at the academy. He hasn't graduated yet, but they're going out on ride-alongs."

When we got to my place, I made a move to pick up the pitchfork I'd tossed in the mad dash to my car. The younger man tried to stop me, probably thinking it was evidence.

I looked from him to O'Malley. "It's mine. I dropped it when I was here before."

"I guess we're lucky no one was here when you first arrived," O'Malley said, "otherwise we'd be looking at a homicide."

Once again, I used the pitchfork to push the door open. This time I let out a scream, dropped the pitchfork, and stumbled back into O'Malley's arms when I saw a figure inside the house, poking through the rubble with a stick.

"Jeez, you could have told me someone was still here," I snapped, pulling away from him.

"I wouldn't have let you skewer him."

I stepped into the entrance of my once cute, now violated, little bungalow. I maneuvered around the cop, and surveyed the damage.

The rug had been pulled up and tossed in a corner on top of a plant called Spanish Dagger. The path to my office was strewn with papers, books, and the contents of drawers. My desktop computer was missing, as was a box of old CDs I normally used as a bookend. All of my clients' files had been rifled, some spilling out of folders, others tossed in a heap in the middle of the floor. My eyes filled with tears; I used my anger to keep them from trickling down my face.

"Who would do this? Why?" My feet shuffled through the papers on the floor as if they were leaves.

I walked through the office to a small room behind it, where I worked out. I couldn't afford a gym membership anymore and had resorted to buying every piece of castoff equipment—including the unused treadmill—that Springfield's secondhand market had to offer. I had a setup that most small-town phys-ed departments would envy.

"Sweet," the young cop said, eyeing my gear.

"And she uses it, too," O'Malley said. "I can attest to that."

"Howl at the moon once." So I had punched him once. It was an accident and there was no permanent damage—his jaw and our relationship, such as it was, had both survived.

"Is the upstairs just as bad?" I asked, hoping for some good news.

"Not nearly," the cop I'd almost pitchforked answered.

I followed O'Malley up the tight spiral staircase in the middle of the house to my tiny bedroom. It was a shambles. The dresser drawers had been pulled out and my clothing obviously handled. The bed had been stripped.

"I'd hate to see your apartment," I told the cop.

"You've still got your sense of humor," O'Malley said. "That's good."

"I just meant that nothing seemed damaged," the younger cop mumbled, embarrassed.

They walked me into the kitchen, where it was more of the same, except the dishwasher and the fridge had been left open. I skidded on a puddle of water near the fridge, O'Malley slipped an arm around me to keep me vertical, then retreated to a more appropriate back pat.

"This was not your garden-variety break-in," O'Malley said. "Our man seems to have been looking for something in particular."

"In my fridge? Like what? Did they think I had money stashed in there like that guy in Washington?" I asked.

"Does anything other than your computer seem to be missing?" he asked.

"You mean like my jewels and collection of three-thousand-dollar handbags?" I did a quick mental inventory of my possessions—I didn't have much worth stealing. "Is my telescope still here?" The cops followed as I ran out to my deck. There it was. Other than my car, the most expensive thing I owned was parked on the deck facing true north. I collapsed onto an old deck chair.

"So why would anyone break in, trash my house, and take a five-year-old desktop? You can probably find newer models at the Salvation Army."

"It's not the computer," O'Malley said. "It's probably what they think is on it."

Fourteen

"Believe me, there's nothing on that computer except old con-
tracts and my iTunes library. If someone broke in here for that,
they'd better like Bruce Springsteen."

That was the mantra I'd repeated five or six times in slightly
differing versions until Mike O'Malley shepherded his two young
fledglings out of my house and down to Springfield's police head-
quarters to file their reports.

The task of putting my house back together was daunting,
but like most unpleasant jobs, you just had to start and with
any luck the process would take over. The entrance was easy—
replace the rug and pad, pick up the overturned pots, sweep up
the Spanish moss and pebble soil covers that had spilled onto
the rough slate tiles. The young cop was right; it was a mess,
but there was no permanent damage. It was just an illustration
of something O'Malley had told me over a year ago: Springfield
has everything the big city has. Including thieves.

Two hours into my cleanup Mike O'Malley returned bearing gifts—a two-liter bottle of Fresca and a pepperoni pizza.

"Looks better already," he said, checking my progress. "Take a break." In my office, he moved stacks of papers to put the pie down on a low wicker chest I normally used as a file cabinet. I went to the kitchen for glasses, plates, and napkins.

There was only one chair in the office and neither of us took it, opting to sit on the floor instead. With some difficulty, O'Malley sat cross-legged on the rug, then popped open the cardboard box and tore off a slice of pizza.

"Good food takes time," he said, motioning for me to join him. I did, and he launched into his theory. The same one he'd been hammering away at before he left.

"You're like a tick, once you get your teeth into something, you don't let go, do you? I repeat, there's no information on my computer that is of any value to anyone. It was of dubious value when it was current. Now it's just a bunch of old files I've been too busy to delete and the music, which I haven't had time to transfer to my laptop," I said. I held my slice point down to let the excess oil drip onto the waxed paper in the pizza box.

"Maybe some documentary you worked on?" he pressed.

"Please. I was hardly an investigative reporter." I'd been vague about my former job. Not that there was anything to hide, but when people hear television, they automatically have you immersed in some political intrigue or hobnobbing with George Clooney when in reality most media jobs are just as mundane as any others. "Let me think. There *was* that time I let myself be embedded at a designer knockoff shop. That might be it."

"Paula, professional thieves don't steal clunky machines. They take small high-ticket items that are easy to fence. That means sell."

"I know what fence means. I watch television. So he was an amateur. He didn't find anything, so he got pissed off, trashed my place, and took the only thing he thought had value." I paraphrased what Babe had told me as if it came from my own vast experience. "Listen, someone broke into my apartment in Brooklyn once and didn't find valuables. Know what he took? Aviator sunglasses and a jar of peanut butter. You think all crooks are smart?"

"Have you discovered anything else that's missing?"

"I haven't checked my canned goods, but to the naked eye, nothing major." The wisecracking had escalated into snapping. This was another cycle we went through. We start out nice, he brings me food, and we end up fighting. It had happened before and I tried to avoid it this time.

"Tell me again what you think," I said, stripping the pepperoni off a second slice and trying my best to strip the sarcasm from my voice.

"I think our man—or woman—planned this carefully. He made sure to come when neither you nor Anna was here."

"Well," I interrupted, "that's a neat trick right there, because even *I'm* not sure when she's going to be here . . . she shows up when she feels like it."

"Be quiet and let me finish," O'Malley said. "They knew when to come and they were looking for something. Information, from the looks of all these papers strewn about. On paper, or a disk, or a flash drive. So the question is, what do you know?"

"I don't know jack. Why do people keep thinking I know something?"

O'Malley put his pizza down and wiped his hands carefully on a wad of paper napkins. He balled them up and tossed them onto his plate. He tented his fingers. "Who else thinks you know something?"

I told O'Malley what had happened at Titans.

"When were you planning to share this information?"

"There are actually two or three things that have happened to me in the past year that I haven't disclosed to the authorities. *It didn't come up,*" I said, exasperated. "Besides, what does that . . . Oh, you're crazy. I talked to that guy for ten, fifteen minutes tops in a hotel bar. What happened to him has nothing to do with me."

"What happened to him was that he got his brains blown out. Maybe you and your girlfriend should be more careful the next time you decide to cruise bars." O'Malley unfolded his legs and stood up. He helped himself to a sheet of paper from my now disconnected printer and took a pen from the flowerpot on my desk. "What did you say his name was?"

"I didn't, but it was Vigoriti. I'm not sure how to spell it. First name, Nick. And we weren't cruising bars, not that it's any business of yours."

"And the cop's name?" he continued, ignoring my protestations of purity.

"Winters." I couldn't tell if he was mad because I'd withheld information, or because he imagined me picking up guys at a hotel bar. Either way, he wasn't happy.

"Local or state?"

"How would I know?"

"What was he wearing?"

"*She* was wearing an ugly blue suit."

"Sounds local."

"Why? The state guys get to wear Armani?"

"Do me a favor," he said, writing down this new info and folding the sheet of paper into quarters. "Set your security alarm tonight. Chances are, whoever it was won't be back, but do it. Promise me, okay?"

We exchanged stiff, formal good nights for two people who'd just been sitting on the floor eating pizza together like a couple of teenagers in a messy dorm, and I gave the door that little extra push it always needed, to make sure the lock caught. In New York, it would have taken two full minutes to throw all the deadbolts and connect all the chains I needed in my old apartment, and you still couldn't keep the bad guys out if they really wanted in. Here it was different. Or so I thought.

From somewhere, I heard the muffled sound of another text message coming in. I worried that I'd created a monster and Caroline Sturgis would be texting me every time she got another bright idea about how to change her garden, her marriage, or her life. I fished around in my bag but couldn't find the phone, then I remembered I'd left it in my pocket after calling the cops. I ran back to my office to get my jacket, but was too late. I entered my code and retrieved the message. *Two brothers. Duct tape. Don't tell anyone.*

Fifteen

Two brothers. The last time Lucy hung out with two brothers, she told me about it at great length over outrageously priced vodka at a bar in NYC's meatpacking district. As I recall, they were named Jesse and Frank. No duct tape was involved and a good time was had by all. But this message felt different.

I don't know how long I stood there trying to figure out what to do. Once, when I was a bookstore manager, we received a tele-phoned bomb threat. For an instant I froze, then I flashed the lights in the store and tried frantically to get the customers to leave. But it was in New York, pre-9/11, so of course they ig-nored me. Nothing happened, and I always wondered where the bastards were, watching me run around like a lunatic and laugh-ing their asses off. I had that same feeling as I stared at my phone.

If Lucy had sent her message fifteen minutes earlier, O'Malley would still have been here. He would have seen the deer-in-the-headlights expression that was undoubtedly on my face, and would have known what to do. I didn't.

I called up the saved message on the phone and stared at it again, finally thinking to hit reply. *Where are you?* I keyed in, and waited for an answer. I paced back and forth, jiggling the phone as if to shake out an answer. The phone beeped; another message was coming in. *Don't know not more than forty minutes from hotel two brothers DON'T TEXT UNLESS I DO FIRST L*

Holy shit. Could she be a little more cryptic? Was she in trouble or was she bragging?

Forty minutes from the hotel wasn't helpful. I'd only been there once. It was on the outskirts of a small town about two blocks long. What was I supposed to do, go to the post office and put up her picture? Shit. I wouldn't tell the cops for now, it could still be an assignation, but I had to tell someone and get a second opinion. I stepped over the piles of papers in my office, grabbed my keys, and went to see my closest adviser, the one person in Springfield I did consider the *F* word, a friend.

"And for my money, that's the best way to contest a speeding ticket. I've done it three or four times," she said, hands on hips and arching her back the tiniest bit. "What are they gonna *say?*"

"We don't all look like you, Babe," said a doughy, blond guy with a baby face. "I'm not sure it would have the same effect coming from someone like me." Most of Babe's audience nodded their heads in agreement. A few customers in the diner seemed dubious, but I was willing to bet they'd resurrect whatever advice she was dispensing if the situation arose.

I closed the door behind me and looked for a booth near the

window. "Hey, Paula. Have a seat over here. Earl's just leaving. He's going to traffic court tomorrow. I was giving him some pointers."

Earl struck me as the kind of guy who didn't normally get this much attention from a beautiful woman and I wouldn't have been surprised if he'd made up the traffic-court story just to have an opening gambit with Babe.

I climbed onto the counter stool recently vacated and left uncomfortably warm by the pudgy Earl; I slid over to the next seat. Babe poured me a coffee and gave me a long look as if she once again knew there was something on my mind. "Take a number," she whispered, leaning in. "Look at these guys. I've already found one a new mechanic and told another how to cure his wife's imaginary migraines."

The rest of Earl's erstwhile legal team hung around for another fifteen minutes debating the merits of Babe's advice despite the fact that she'd given them all bills, her tacit signal that the conversation was over. I nursed my coffee and waited for them to leave. When they didn't, Babe piled a few homemade sugar donuts onto a plate and led me by the arm to a booth at the back of the diner.

"Alba, take over the counter, okay?" Alba did as she was told, happy to play understudy for her idol.

"They take much?" she asked, pulling off a piece of donut. "Do you need any dough? We were hit once, years ago. I've got protection now." She jerked her head in the direction of the counter, or maybe it was outside, across the street where the police substation was.

I shook my head. "It's not about the robbery." I wasn't sure how much to tell her. I was lousy at asking for help and I didn't want to involve her if this turned out to be something serious.

"A friend of mine is in trouble," I started.

"First off, that's good. Not good, but at least it's not you. Who is it? The one with the philandering husband? No, don't tell me. Let's keep this abstract."

Babe lived for this—she genuinely loved solving other people's problems. In another lifetime she might have been a radio shrink.

"Most problems are either money or men. Okay, your friend's a woman and she's having man trouble," she said, waiting for confirmation.

"Sort of." I started to think this was a bad idea. What if I didn't like what Babe had to say? What if she said *Call the cops now, you idiot!?* "She may be in a place where she doesn't want to be," I said, dragging my feet.

Babe looked puzzled. "Literally or figuratively?"

"Could be both."

"I hate it when the answer is *both,*" she said, shaking her head and frowning.

Over Babe's shoulder I saw the door open and three of Springfield's finest come in, including Mike O'Malley. Babe turned around to see who I was staring at. "Stay right here," she said. "I give out better advice than a bartender. I'll be right back, I'm just going to go seat those guys. Alba's got her hands full."

Babe led the cops to a booth just ten feet away and it made me realize the Paradise was not the best place for a private conversation. O'Malley excused himself and came over to where I was sitting.

"Ms. Holliday, I thought it was Chinese food that had you hungry an hour later, not pizza. Have you thought of something else that might help us with your break-in?"

It took me five full seconds to answer. I looked from O'Malley to Babe and back to O'Malley. "No," I lied.

Sixteen

Within an hour, I'd gone home and packed, sticking a pair of black leather pants, dressy shoes, and a sleeveless top in my bag, in case I needed to pass myself off as a regular guest at the Titans Hotel. Then I hit the road, stopping only to fill the tank.

Babe and Pete were just closing up as I sped by the Paradise. For the briefest of moments I considered pulling in to get a reality check, but I left my foot on the gas and kept on going.

I was feeling half tired and half wired. There was no way I'd have gotten any sleep after Lucy's message—especially in a house recently pillaged by someone who was likely a thief, a psycho, or at best, a garden-variety creep. Two weird things I could pass off as coincidence, but three was pushing it. I wouldn't have connected Nick's death with the break-in at my house if O'Malley hadn't planted the seed. And now, Lucy's obscure message. What the hell was it that people seemed to think I knew?

When you're consciously looking for links you can find them

anywhere, like Nostradamus theories. That side of my brain was now connecting so many dots it wouldn't be long before I convinced myself that this trail would lead me to the remains of Amelia Earhart.

I slid onto the on-ramp and entered the sparse highway traffic with a full tank of gas and a four-pack of diet Red Bull to help me stay awake on the drive to Titans.

My phone was on my lap, plugged into the cigarette lighter and turned to speakerphone on the outside chance that Lucy would call or text-message again. The part about the duct tape was worrying me, but Lucy had a more adventurous sex life than I did. If she was partying, I was going to give her hell. But if she wasn't . . .

Classical music would have put me to sleep so I settled on a college radio station in the middle of its weekly Irish hour. That, the Red Bull, and four open windows were the only things keeping me from pulling over into a deserted weigh station, curling up into a fetal position, and having a snooze. I'm a good sleeper. That's been the consensus with everyone from my mother to my last sweetheart. I know it's supposed to be a compliment, but it's hard to take it as praise when someone tells you they love it when you're unconscious.

Twenty minutes into the drive, I was buzzing on the caffeine and Riverdancing with my shoulders, affecting that haughty head toss that always makes the female dancers look like prancing ponies. The prancing stopped when I passed the gas station/minimarket where I'd had my encounter with the Michelin Man. A cold wave rippled through my body. Was that incident connected, too, or was I just reaching a new level of paranoia? I checked the rearview mirror as if the MM had been camped out on the highway for the past twenty-four hours waiting for me to reappear. I raised the windows and told myself it was just the early spring weather that had given me the chills.

I was chuckling to myself about what an idiot I was being when the phone rang. I jumped a little in my seat, just enough to knock the phone to the floor of the car and make me have to stretch and feel around blindly through old Mapquest directions, loose change, and empty Red Bull cans until I found it.

I wedged the phone between the gearbox and the driver's seat, squinting until I could make out the sender's name. Jon Chappell. I hit answer.

"Hey, what are you doing up at this hour?" I asked.

"I'm no kid, I made it all the way to midnight once."

After all I'd been through, it felt as if it should have been 4:00 A.M., but it was only 11:30.

"Where's my story?" he asked.

"What story?"

"That's what I get for hiring friends. You're fired. The corpse flower story. The one you harangued me to let you cover? The feature that no one is waiting for? I bumped the Hawley family quilt story for you and Hawley Real Estate is a big advertiser."

I'd completely forgotten.

"I may have a bigger story for you," I said, trying to tempt him with something more journalistically challenging than either a plant or the Hawleys' moldy old blanket.

"I heard; we get alerts on that stuff. Sorry for your loss but break-ins are strictly page-fourteen stuff. At the risk of sounding callous, only home invasions make the front page. You gotta be there or it's no story."

"There's a slim chance that the break-in at my place was connected to the murder I told you about at Titans." I dangled a few details of O'Malley's visit and just enough of Lucy's message to pique his interest, but not so much that he'd freak out and get the local cops, the state troopers, and the FBI out looking for her.

"It's also possible Lucy made it up to Titans after all. I'm going back to see."

"Why don't you just call her?" he said.

Because she might be duct-taped to a chair courtesy of Connecticut's answer to the Krays? "I think she's having signal problems." That was one excuse every cell phone user in the state would buy. "I'm driving now, I can't talk anymore."

"Keep me in the loop," he said. "I want the exclusive if this really is a story. And worst case, you better come back with pictures of that damn flower." Just as I hung up, I heard him say that the paper was only going to pay for my mileage once. I didn't want to admit it, but I was glad Jon had called. In the back of my mind, I wanted someone to know where I was going. Just in case.

When I arrived at Titans, the parking attendant was propped up on a plastic storage crate, leaning against a flaking pillar. His legs were stretched out in front of him and he was snoring loudly. One other car, an electric-blue Isuzu festooned with dream catchers and bumper stickers, was parked diagonally in the fifteen-minute registration parking area.

I yanked my bag out of the backseat and the straps caught on the tines of one of the pitchforks I'd bought only that morning. It seemed like days ago. In plain sight with a truckload of other garden tools, a pitchfork is a perfectly reasonable item. On its own, it's faintly creepy, like something from a date-night horror flick. I untangled the straps and tossed one of the small tarps I carried for plant material over the pitchfork.

The parking attendant made no attempt to move, so I tapped

him on the shoulder, and handed over my keys and a couple of dollars. The kid said nothing, and I guessed that meant the tip was too small to warrant a thank-you or even an acknowledgment.

You're welcome. Next time I park it myself.

The weight of the revolving door reminded me just how tired I was. I promised myself a solid six hours of sleep before embarking on what I hoped was a foolish wild-goose chase. I imagined Lucy and me laughing about this over drinks on my deck.

If the outside of the hotel was dead, the inside wasn't much livelier—Titans at two A.M. was not exactly filled with the sound of champagne corks popping, fingers snapping, and high rollers squealing with delight. A few stragglers were holding up the end of the bar I could see from the entrance, and a couple who couldn't keep their hands off each other stumbled over to the elevators.

Bernie Mishkin was also there, head down, locked in a serious conversation with a pretty woman in a puffy fur-trimmed vest. She had sunglasses on top of her head despite the fact that it was nighttime and she was indoors. A deep tan and smoker's lines probably added ten years to someone who probably wasn't that much older than me, but she had a nice, wide smile, and Mishkin seemed charmed.

If Mishkin noticed me, he didn't show it, but it would have been hard for him to let his attention drift from his companion, who had her hand on his knee and was leaning in to either make a point or show him her cleavage. A widower for just a few months, Mishkin looked like he'd already found a replacement for his beloved Fran. Something told me she wasn't the marketing genius that Fran had been, but I had a feeling she was pretty good at something else. The woman flicked a key ring with a blue rubber pompom on it, and periodically pointed with it for effect.

There was one waitress on the floor and a plump brunette with thick, shiny hair and Buddy Holly glasses was manning the bar; I didn't see Oksana. Since bartenders generally knew the locals, and two brothers might have stuck in someone's memory, I decided to summon up enough energy to ask the bartender a few questions before crashing in my room.

I took the long way to the lounge, avoiding Mishkin and circling the corpse flower, which hadn't changed much since my last visit. From the corner of my eye I saw Mishkin's female companion storm out of the lounge area, nearly knocking over three frat boys who'd just come in. Mishkin mopped his brow and straightened his tie, emitting a fake laugh to suggest that nothing major had happened, but the look on his face said otherwise. Mishkin scoped out the room for witnesses to the embarrassing scene, but the few people who'd seen anything were involved in their own dramas and it barely registered. I hid behind the corpse flower, thinking, *Ain't love grand?*

After he left, I settled in at the bar, ordering a drink and a bowl of Goldfish and engaging the bartender in a round of girl talk. Despite what Detective Stacy Winters thought, I hadn't interviewed anyone in a long time. What I remembered about it was that a successful interviewer made the subject feel comfortable, as if you were having a conversation, not grilling him or her under a spotlight. So that's what I did. I nursed a white ginger cosmo and gently complained about my (nonexistent) boss, my (nonexistent) boyfriend, and the paucity of good-looking men at the bar at Titans. By the time she'd topped off her last few customers, it was as if she and I were old friends.

She told me it was Oksana's night off, and Hector Ruiz, the only other person I knew to ask about, had left about an hour earlier.

"Hector and his wife and baby girl live in a mobile park," she volunteered without much prodding. "Near the reservation. A lot of Titans workers do. There's not much affordable housing around here since the casino went up."

"Is that where you live?" I asked, trying to read her name through her long hair. She brushed it back over one shoulder. "Helayne?"

She shook her head, and the hair fell back against her round face. "I moved back in with my family, but I'm going for my aesthetician's license, so I may be out again soon." She made it sound like she'd be crashing out of prison.

"What about Oksana?" I asked.

"She shares with a girl named Nadia. In the same park as Hector. Nadia has a double-wide." Helayne was impressed.

Nadia worked at the big casino. She'd kicked her boyfriend out of their trailer a few months ago and Oksana had moved in to help out with the monthly payments. It was supposed to be temporary.

"O. thought she'd move in with Nick, but he was a big talker. A terrible flirt. He came on to me once, but I told him I was engaged. 'You see that ring?' I said. 'That means something.' You heard what happened to him, right?" she said, under her breath.

I nodded, and spared a moment for the late Nick Vigoriti, who might have been a little less successful with the ladies than I'd originally thought. This was mildly interesting but it wasn't getting me any closer to the two brothers.

"A friend of mine was here last weekend. She said she met some really cute guys. They're a little young for me," I said, tilting my head toward the table of college kids who got rowdier with each round of Guinness and were taking turns trying to get the widget out of the can. "A couple of brothers, I think she said."

Helayne gave it some thought. I couldn't see her in a ménage, but you never knew about people. For all I knew, there was a trapeze over her bed.

"Some brothers, but not single. And no one I'd call cute." She made eye contact with the security guard and motioned toward the kids so that he would keep an eye on them.

"Well, my friend has eclectic taste. You or I might not think they were good-looking." *That's right, we're women of the world.*

"The Laheys are cute, but I think the younger one is gay."

"I don't think that's her thing." I played with the dregs of my drink as long as I could before she brought me a second, stronger than the first.

"The Crawfords are good-looking," she said, setting the drink down. "Billy and Claude. There was a third one but he died. But they're not allowed in here anymore. Something happened, before I was hired. Oksana told me about it. Security has instructions to keep them out. Maybe they drank too much. You should ask her. Oksana knows more male customers than I do."

I bet she did. Oksana's vulnerability and pouty good looks probably got her as much attention as she wanted. Maybe more.

Two Asian guys entered the lounge, ignoring the No Smoking sign and feigning ignorance when the security guard told them to put the cigarettes out. The waitress came back with their orders and Helayne got busy mixing their drinks. "They stare as if they've never seen boobs before, but they're good tippers," the waitress said.

I toyed with the idea of waiting for Helayne to finish, but the drinks and the hour were conspiring to get me in the sack. Tomorrow I'd face Oksana and ask her about the Crawford brothers.

The phone rang at around 3:30 A.M. I must have just fallen asleep because I woke up with a start, the way you do when you're afraid you've nodded off in an inappropriate place like the theater or a meeting. I looked around trying to remember where I was and where the hell that obnoxious noise was coming from. I knocked over the lamp and a water bottle reaching for the phone and caught it on its sixth ring.

"Hello," I mumbled into the dead air. "Lucy, is that you?" I turned on the light and saw the last drops of a two-liter bottle of water trickling into my Nikes.

"Do you know a woman named Lucy?" someone asked, surprised.

"Who is this?" I raised myself up on my elbows, waiting for an answer.

"It's me. Oksana. The bartender?"

"Oksana, it's . . ." The numbers on the digital clock were magnified and distorted by the overturned bottle; I shoved it aside. "It's three-thirty. What is it?"

"I need you to help me find out what happened to Nick," she said.

"I have no idea what happened to Nick." I sat on the edge of the bed and shook the water out of my shoes. "Do *you* know a woman named Lucy?" I asked.

She paused, as if she was deciding how much to tell me. "We can't talk on the hotel phone. Will you meet me at the casino?"

"Now?"

"Yes."

"Why?"

"The night Nick was killed, he left the bar to meet a woman named Lucy."

Seventeen

My sneakers were soaked, so I slipped into the only other shoes I'd packed—the heels I brought to wear with my leather pants. As I dressed, I started to feel like a hooker making a house call, but it was either my *nice* outfit or cargo pants with heels and that would have been too weird, even for me.

Unlike his counterpart at Titans, the parking attendant at the casino was cheerful and energetic; at that hour of the morning it was downright creepy to be so perky.

"Welcome to happy Hunting Ridge, ma'am." He said it as if "happy" was part of the casino's full name. "Have you been with us before?"

I wanted to tell him that I wasn't *with* Hunting Ridge and would probably never be and that the last time I was out at 4 A.M. it was with a flashlight and I was looking for slugs, but this time I was meeting a probably delusional woman who thought she knew something about a murder and a kidnapping. But I decided to spare both of us. I forced a toothless smile and fished out a five, hoping for a better reaction than I'd gotten from the attendant at Titans.

"Don't bury it. I won't be long," I said, handing him the folded bill. "Know where the Coyote Café is?"

"Yes, ma'am." He beamed, eager to be of service. I couldn't remember the last time five dollars had provoked such a rapturous response. "Straight in, past the Chilulhy sculpture, then make a left. Have a lucky stay!"

Jeez, what did they put in the water here?

If I was expecting to see glamorous model types and men in tuxedos playing baccarat and passing the shoe, I would have been sorely disappointed. I'd been to Vegas plenty of times when I was in the television business, and although it had changed dramatically in the years since, there was still a frisson of rat-pack glamour if you looked hard enough for it.

Not at Hunting Ridge. The exuberant use of wood, slate, and river stones gave the place the look of an upscale lodge with incongruously placed slot machines and designer boutiques—Chanel and Cavalli sharing space with Squanto and Sacajawea. There were any number of ways to leave your money there.

The Coyote Café's sandwich-board menu was bordered with a blanket pattern and offered, among other things, Chippewa chips and Navajo pancakes. I didn't know where the Chippewas came from, but we were a good two thousand miles from any Navajos. Oksana was behind the sign, pacing and chewing her nails. Then she spotted me.

"It's too crowded in there," she said, walking over to me. "Come this way."

"Oksana. I'm running on fumes. What's all this about? What do you know about my friend Lucy?"

She pulled me over to a bench near a diorama of a Native American village. Every few minutes one of the resin natives offered resin corn to a resin settler who looked suspiciously like Brad Pitt.

"Was she your friend?"

A chill crept through me. "What do you mean, *was* she?"

Eighteen

Oksana played with a pack of cigarettes but didn't open it. She fiddled with her flat, dirty blond hair, the scarf that was wrapped around her neck three or four times, and the hem of her skirt.

"Hector told me your name and I Googled you. The newspaper article said you helped solve a crime once. Is that why you're here?"

"The police solve crimes. I'm a gardener. I have to be honest with you. I'm not here because of Nick, I'm only here because you mentioned someone named Lucy. She's the person I was waiting for the night I met Nick in the bar."

Oksana shook her head back and forth like a petulant child.

"What do you mean, no? I know what I was doing there."

"The other woman met Nick . . . and now he's dead."

Nick had gotten two phone calls after I left and Oksana had heard him speak to someone he called Lucy. He said he'd meet her.

"He made a joke about older women and then he left. That was the last time I ever saw him." Older women? Lucy was thirty-five. I guess if you were Oksana's age, that was old.

She looked around again, as if she expected someone to be listening over her shoulder. I dropped my voice just in case.

"Why are you doing that? Who else would care what we're talking about?"

"There are people."

Now she was weirding me out. "Do you by any chance know a couple of guys, the Crawford brothers?" I asked.

Oksana nodded. "They're natives. They were friends with Nick."

Maybe Lucy met all three of them. But why wouldn't she have text messaged that, instead of . . . *two brothers?*

"Did you see them last night at the hotel?" I asked.

"No, they can't come in. They picketed some cheesy Indian display the Mishkins put up outside the hotel. Worse than this one," she said, pointing to the marginally distasteful one right near us. "Rachel got the cops to kick them out and a judge to say that they couldn't come back. I don't think Nick liked it either. He told me that's what he and the Mishkins argued about."

"Are you sure?"

"Nick said they were greedy."

"Do you know what he meant?"

She shook her head and looked around again.

"Who are you expecting to see?" I asked, exasperated.

Wide-eyed, she leaned in and whispered the name.

"Sergei."

Nineteen

Sergei Russianoff was an entrepreneurial Ukrainian who had helped Oksana out of the orphanage in Kiev, where she grew up. After she watched her stepfather and mother drink themselves to death, Oksana and her younger brother went to live with their grandmother, but the old woman could only afford to look after one child and for practical reasons she chose the little boy. That sent Oksana to the orphanage until she reached the age of seventeen, when all residents were booted out, sometimes into the arms of mobsters or predators.

Russianoff was neither. He recruited girls in Kiev to come to the U.S. to work in his various small businesses in Connecticut.

"I'd visited with a host family in Connecticut when I lived in the orphanage. American families would take us for three weeks. We would get off the plane with a plastic bag that held one change of underwear. For those three weeks we had everything . . . as much food as we wanted, television, toys. Some people bought us clothes or books. One time I stayed with a couple that had a dog. It was like a dream. Then we got shipped home and we woke up. Most of the time any gifts we were allowed to take home were stollen by the older kids. When Sergei said I could live in Connecticut, it was as if he told me I was going to Hollywood to be a movie star."

She didn't become a movie star. Sergei trained her to be a dog groomer. For the first time since I'd met her, she smiled, and it made her look like the young girl she still was.

Russianoff had a house in Bridgeport where they'd all lived. At times there were as many as twelve of them. Oksana said it was like the orphanage only they had better clothing and didn't have to go outside to smoke.

"Another older girl, Sveta, and I would drive around and give dog baths in the back of a van." Now I knew where Sveta had gotten her training. I must have felt like a big old Great Dane to her.

I'd seen other dog-grooming vehicles tooling around Springfield and thought the idea was ingenious. But Sergei's company had had a few mishaps. The owner of a golden retriever that had gotten a particularly bad haircut sued. She didn't win, but things went south after that.

"The dog's coat grew back, she didn't have to ruin him," Oksana said.

We walked through the casino's arcade, absentmindedly looking into shop windows, although most of the shops were closed.

"Did you get paid?" I asked.

"We got an allowance."

What a guy. In addition to the mobile dog-grooming company, Sergei had a small bar, a housecleaning service, and an employment agency. But apparently his big dream was to open a skating rink. Not just a place where suburban kids would go to flirt and drink hot chocolate on a Friday night, but a full-scale facility where coaches and former champions would go to train.

Oksana lowered her voice. "He borrowed a lot of money. He thought he could get a famous skater like Viktor Petrenko to endorse it, but it didn't work out. I think Petrenko opened his own place."

"So what happened?" I asked.

"Now he has to pay the mortgage on a big empty building that he can't sell, with a secondhand Zamboni that doesn't work."

That could be a problem—not much call for Zambonis on eBay. So Sergei got into other businesses. Oksana didn't elaborate, but the other businesses sounded suspiciously like an escort service and small-scale loan-sharking. She said she didn't want to work for him anymore and I wasn't surprised. When some housecleaning clients started to miss items from their homes Sergei caught the attention of the local authorities. Nothing was ever proven, but now he was on their radar.

"I shouldn't be talking about this. I would never do anything to hurt Sergei. But he is nervous that I will." She looked pretty nervous herself.

She wrestled with how much more to tell me. Her tiny face screwed up until she looked like a toddler about to break into a tantrum, but she held back.

The roommate had dropped her off at the casino and had just started her shift, so Oksana asked for a lift home. It was nearing five and I had passed the point of being up late and was now up early, so I said sure. I was disappointed Oksana hadn't seen Lucy at the hotel, but at least I could follow up on the Crawford brothers.

Surprisingly, there was still a decent-size crowd at the casino—stragglers, Ambien zombies, groups of guys that might have been bachelor parties, sleep-deprived vacationers, and more than a few manic souls still looking for that lucky slot machine with their name on it—more people than Titans probably had on a holiday weekend in the summer.

We made our way back to the lobby. Then Oksana spotted two men at the end of the long hallway and visibly stiffened. She pulled me into one of the Native American boutiques in the casino that was still open—turquoise jewelry 24/7.

One of the guys was skinny with long, greasy blond hair. I couldn't see the other one that well because the resin Native Americans had gone into their timed routine again, handing out fake corn and receiving fake trinkets from the fake settlers. All I could make out was that he was a large man wearing a leather jacket.

Oksana was slim enough to hide behind a rack of oversize fringed bags while I pretended to be shopping for silver cuffs. She stood stock-still until the men passed.

"Are they gone?" she whispered, terrified.

I nodded. Now I was as paralyzed as she was. The heavy one was the Michelin Man.

Twenty

The Michelin Man's name was Vitaly. His skinny friend was
Marat and could have been the guy I saw smoking outside of Titans. In happier times Oksana had innocently asked them their
last names and they had told her that anyone who needed their
last names to find them could go screw themselves. Charming.

"Why are they following you and why in the world would the
fat one have been following me?" I asked.

"We can't talk here," she whispered.

I thought she was being melodramatic but who knew? I told
the salesclerk we were trying to avoid some creeps who weren't
taking no for an answer and asked her to look outside to see if the
two men were still there. Once she was convinced that we weren't
plotting to rip her off, she did it. Then she pointed to a house
phone, where I called the valet to get my car. Oksana took off her
scarf, borrowed my quilted jacket, and bought a two-dollar bandanna with a dice and feathers pattern on it. She tied it around

her head in a makeshift disguise and we walked out of the shop expecting to feel a hand on our shoulders at any moment.

By the time we got to the entrance we were breathing easier. My car was already there and we took off for the trailer park, where Oksana and her roommate lived. It wasn't far but Oksana took me by the back roads and I tried to imprint the turns and landmarks so I'd be able to get back without her.

"Isn't there a more direct way?" I asked, faintly irritated.

"This is the way Nadia comes. It's the only way I know," she said.

"All right, we're out of there. Now why is Sergei having his men follow you and why would they have been following me? This can't be about some petty thefts from last year."

"Vitaly protects Sergei. Sergei is somehow involved with the Mishkins' investors. I don't know how, but the night Nick was killed, I overheard him tell someone on the phone he could make it uncomfortable for people if they didn't find a way to cut him in. Vitaly was at the bar. He also heard what Nick said." She looked down at her nail-bitten hands and tore off a piece of cuticle. I waited for the other shoe to drop.

"What else?"

"I might have told him Nick had mentioned an older woman. He might have thought I meant you."

Older woman? When did I join the ranks of older women? I was in my thirties, for Pete's sake. What was I supposed to do, flick my hair and inject the word *like* into every other sentence?

"Did you tell Vitaly about Lucy's call?"

"I may have," she said quietly.

And now Nick was dead, my house had been ransaked, and Lucy was missing. But why?

We were on a poorly lit road riddled with enough potholes to make it seem like an obstacle course. "Oksana, are we getting close?"

"The building up ahead on the left, that's the manager's office. He's never there, and the gate is always open. Just make a left and turn into the park." So much for a gated community.

Oksana used the word *park* loosely. In the near dark I could make out rows of similarly shaped trailers reminiscent of overseas shipping containers and vintage diners. Occasionally one would stand out because of its outlandish paint job, or the disemboweled vehicle on the rectangle of outdoor space each tenant had a right to—I tried to remember them as breadcrumbs to help me get out of there after I'd dropped her off.

The only sign of vegetation was a few rows down, an aluminum Christmas tree one of the occupants had placed outside of the trailer, bits of tinsel still attached and fluttering in the early-morning breeze despite the fact that it was mid-March.

"Turn right at that tree."

I had a feeling if the tree was moved Oksana wouldn't know how to get home any more than she knew how to get there from the casino. It was all done by rote. We pulled up to the double-wide and she got out.

"Look after yourself," I said.

Twenty-one

I zigzagged out of the trailer park using the landmarks I'd remembered—a peace sign made of minilights, a kids' jungle gym, and finally the aluminum Christmas tree close to the entrance. I used the same strategy when I left the pockmarked road that had led to Oksana's, trying to make my way back to the casino.

It should have been easier as the sun was coming up, but it wasn't. Buildings and things I hadn't seen thirty minutes earlier materialized and made me doubt my route selection. A convenience store came up on the right, a small gray shack that looked like a prefab army building with a blue neon Miller sign I would have remembered. It confirmed that I'd missed my turn. I hung a U-turn to slowly retrace my steps.

Jeez, it was a huge hotel—I could faintly see it in the distance through the morning haze—I just couldn't seem to find the road that led there. I crawled back and stopped two hundred yards ahead of a turn I didn't make, just in time to see a silvery blue sedan take a left and pull onto the long stretch of road that led to the trailer park. I hadn't seen another vehicle since Oksana and I had left the casino and I was startled by the appearance of another car.

I told myself it was probably another waitress or pit boss who'd just finished his shift at the casino. All the same, I killed the lights and rolled into a hidden driveway. If the driver of the other car looked in his rearview mirror all he'd see was a dark bump behind a hemlock tree, not a nervous woman wondering if the two men who'd just driven by were Ukrainian mobsters.

All I could see were shadows. The driver's silhouette was the larger of the two. But that could have been anyone—a woman in a fur coat, a guy in a down jacket—it didn't have to be the Michelin Man. And just because he was on the road to Oksana's place didn't mean he was headed there. But I felt sure it was the men we'd seen at the casino, and they were looking for Oksana, or the two of us.

With the engine turned off all the heat had left the car and I sat there, a chill setting in, wondering what to do next. *Do I go back to Oksana's to see if she is okay? What could I do if she wasn't?*

Stacy Winters's card was still floating around in the bottom of my bag, but by the time I found it, I'd talked myself out of calling her. What would I say? Two people I didn't see may be visiting a person I barely know?

I started the car slowly, with a KISS. *Key, ignition, seatbelt, signal.* An old boyfriend told me that when he taught me how to drive and I still thought of it—a lifelong habit started by a boyfriend of a hundred days. By the time I got to *signal,* I saw the headlights of a car racing toward me. The same car, with the same two passengers. The stocky driver made the turn that I had missed minutes before and luckily he didn't notice the Jeep backing out of the hidden driveway.

Rather than get on the road behind them, I kept my lights off and slowly navigated the rutted dirt road they'd just left until I pulled into the trailer park and found my way back to Oksana's.

When I got there, she was gone.

Twenty-two

"Someone you drove home isn't there? Is that really why you're calling me at this ungodly hour?"

Detective Stacy Winters was lucky I hung up the first time I called, almost two hours earlier.

No one had answered at Oksana's place and repeatedly calling her name before six A.M. got me nothing but angry responses from her neighbors. The loudest was the guy with the peace sign. I drove to the casino, and from there back to Titans, checking the rearview mirror so often I nearly missed the exit for the hotel.

I should have been exhausted but too much information was coming at me all at once and I needed to talk to someone about what, if anything, all of this meant. When I finally broke down and called Winters, I spilled everything I knew about Lucy's disappearance, Oksana's story, the Crawford brothers, and the Ukrainians.

"Look, I know I told you to call me if you thought of anything else, but lots of times we just say that. We don't really think you're going to call us. If we thought you really knew anything about Vigoriti's murder we'd still be questioning you."

Stacy Winters was in no danger of being burdened with either a warm bedside manner or an insatiable curiosity. Even after I told her about Nick's involvement with the Mishkins and the Crawford brothers.

"Nick was always claiming he knew more than he did," she said, unimpressed. "He should have gone into politics. With his looks and shtick he could have been governor. You don't have to be smart, you get all the dates you want, and you get to rub shoulders with big-time criminals—not the small fry Nick usually hung out with." I could hear her slurp a drink and rustle a few papers in the background.

"Look, you're what? A gardener? Go plant some tulips and leave the police work to the professionals."

What was her obsession with tulips? Was that the only plant she knew? I was tempted to tell her you don't plant tulips in the spring, but somehow I knew it wouldn't be received as the scathing criticism I meant it to be, so I didn't respond.

"What about my friend Lucy? I haven't spoken to her in two days."

"I've got friends I haven't heard from in ten years," she said. Big surprise.

"What was her last message? *Two men . . .* ? She could have been sending you a joke—*Two men walk into a bar.*"

"Why would she have called Nick twice?" I said.

"How should I know? Maybe she was asking him to bring the K-Y jelly. We don't know that she did call him twice. Or even once. Oksana Smolova is what we in law enforcement refer to as an unreliable source."

She told me Oksana had been picked up for soliciting three years ago when she was still a teenager, bailed out by a local dirtbag who claimed to be her guardian.

"Sweet old Uncle Sergei, that nice man with the doggies."

Apparently, Oksana and Sergei had had a falling out when she went to work at Titans. She failed to catch the eye of the newly widowed Bernie Mishkin, who they both assumed was rolling in dough; then she latched on to Nick Vigoriti.

"Never one to say no to the horizontal hora, Nick took her out a few times, then they cooled off. At least he did. She was still looking for that sugar daddy or meal ticket. You know you're lucky she didn't lead you into a trap where some of her Ukrainian buddies slapped you around. Or worse."

Winters let the words hang in the air for effect. I couldn't have been so wrong about Oksana. That girl was terrified. Still, she did admit to telling the Michelin Man about me. Was he the one who'd ransacked my place? And she'd told him about Lucy. I'd called all of Lucy's numbers a dozen times since her first text message. Where the hell was she?

According to Winters, Lucy wasn't considered one of the missing. If you're over the age of eighteen in the state of Connecticut and there doesn't appear to be any evidence of foul play, you're just *gone*.

"So how long does she have to be *gone* before she's missing?"

"You're not listening. It's not a time thing. No evidence of a crime, no missing person."

"So, poof, someone's gone, just like that?" I asked.

"Just like that."

Twenty-three

I didn't have so many friends that I could afford to have even one of them go poof. Since I'd moved to the 'burbs I'd discovered who my real friends were. The party crowd in New York, the business acquaintances I'd kept on speed dial because they owed me a favor—those guys were gone. Lucy was the only one from my past who was more than the occasional drinks, e-mail, or Christmas card friend.

I had a hard time believing what Detective Winters had told me about missing persons in Connecticut. I preferred to think she was just a bitch on wheels with some as-yet-unknown agenda so I grabbed a Diet Coke from the minibar, powered up my laptop, and went online to do my own research. I soon learned everything Winters had told me was true.

There were more than one hundred thousand missing persons in the United States, seven hundred in Connecticut alone. And if you weren't a child under the age of eighteen, or a senior, you could very easily just go *poof*. One poor woman in Connecticut was still so heartsick over her son's disappearance that she'd been paying for a billboard with his picture on it for eight years.

Without evidence of a crime there was no state or local law addressing missing adults, only children or at-risk adults with diminished mental capacity or health problems. I didn't think I could sell Lucy as diminished capacity, and her only health issues were that she'd now missed three krav maga workouts and pretty soon her roots would start showing.

In this neck of the woods, you had a better chance of getting a stolen car found than a healthy thirty-four-year-old woman.

Wait a minute, that could work.

In New York City a stolen car wouldn't get much of a rise out of the police, but in Connecticut it was tantamount to stealing someone's horse in the Old West. If Lucy's car was found at a ski resort in Vermont, I would simply drive there and brain her for making me go through all of this. If it wasn't, well, I'd deal with that if it happened.

Lucy shared an assistant with another producer. The few times I'd spoken with the girl she sounded like any one of the overworked twenty somethings I remembered from my former career—in the office by eight A.M., at her desk until eight or nine P.M., and on call 24/7 waiting for her first credit, her first break. Smart, ambitious kids who would gleefully step over their boss's broken and bleeding body if it meant they'd be included in a programming meeting or get sent to the Sundance festival. I called Lucy's office again.

As she was taught, the assistant picked up after three rings. I chose my words carefully. *Lucy had asked me to call, she'd misplaced the keys to her rental car. Did the assistant have an 800 number for the rental car company?* All the best lies are short and sweet. Once you start explaining too much you get into trouble. There'd be no long-winded explanation of how that wacky Lucy had lost the keys juggling a champagne bottle and her BagBorroworSteal purse in the hot-air balloon she'd taken off in with a handsome Australian pilot. Keep the lie short and sweet.

"It's 1-800-YO-DRIVE." *Click.* That was easy. Since I could no longer further her career, the assistant didn't feel the need to chat with me any longer than absolutely necessary.

YoDrive was a small private company near Lucy's office that extended special long-term rates to KCPS staffers. I'd used them myself back in the day. The next lie might be harder since a diligent employee could justifiably be worried about the company's property and ask questions I didn't want to answer.

I needn't have worried. Remembering what a tiny office it was I intentionally waited until lunchtime to call, in the hopes that whoever answered the phone would be distracted—either by his takeout order arriving or because he was shorthanded at the desk. I was right.

The lying was coming easier now; I guess some skill sets you never lose. This time I was calling from a sister station in Massachusetts. *I needed Lucy's vehicle info and license plate number to make sure that she didn't get towed when she arrived tomorrow and parked in our small visitors lot.* It was weak, but I delivered my lines with just the right touch of boredom to suggest that I really was who I said I was. Never underestimate the ability of a disinterested employee to give you information.

Lucy was driving a white 2007 Subaru standard SUV with Rhode Island plates, 475 LMP. I'd simply report the car stolen. That way the police would have to look for her. Or at least her car.

I called it in to the local police telling them the last time I saw it it was at the Titans Hotel. I gave them my cell phone as a contact number. It was all I could do at the moment. The moment being one where I'd had three hours of sleep and finally started to feel it.

After a shower and some zzz's, I'd try to see Bernie Mishkin again. Some of what Oksana had told me made me think that his investment opportunity was at the heart of a number of mysteries at Titans, and maybe even Lucy's unexplained absence.

I went into the bathroom, turned on the shower, and peeled off my clothes. Hands on sink, I stood there with the steam filling up the room, inspecting my face in the mirror. I looked worse than I thought I would.

After thirty they say sleep and sex are the best beauty secrets, and I wasn't getting much of either. Having a seasonal business or job always sounds good to those people who don't have one. They only think of the time off, not the time spent planning, the financial crunch, and the plain uncertainty of things you can't control, like pests and the weather. I was getting a taste of what farmers must go through, and it was keeping me up at nights.

Lucy had been trying to nudge me back into the television business for the past year until, as she put it, I "got this thing out of my system." But I had a five-year plan for Dirty Business. If I was still treading water in five years I'd give it up and go back to TV.

"Dream on," Lucy had said. "I can hold your seat at the table for a while, but this next generation is carnivorous. I can't stand still for a minute without half a dozen assistants breathing down my neck."

That was the attitude that made me still cling to the possibility she was chasing down a story. But it was the likelier possibility that she wasn't that was giving me the worried, haggard look

I saw in the mirror. I splashed some water on my face and brushed my teeth. Mercifully the steam began to obscure my reflection. Just then I felt someone's presence outside, in my room.

I covered up with a towel and quietly closed the bathroom door, pressing my ear against the door, straining to hear who it might be. With the shower on and the door closed I couldn't hear a thing so I pushed the button on the doorknob and held the door with my left foot, against the intruder I was sure was just about to burst in. I reached out with my right arm and stretched to turn off the shower. Of course the towel fell. My reflection in the cloudy mirror showed a woman practicing yoga for spastics—sun salutation meets pratfall.

With the water turned off I definitely heard someone outside. There was nothing in the bathroom I could use to protect myself but I remembered that the lamp I'd knocked over the night before was just a few feet from the bathroom door. If necessary, it was thin enough and light enough for me to yank out of the wall and use as a club. As long as the intruder didn't have a gun. If he had a gun the lamp probably wouldn't work, but I had to think positive. I picked up the towel, unlocked the door, and cracked it open an inch. I heard something snapping. I opened the door another inch.

Twenty-four

With her iPod on, the housekeeper hadn't heard a thing. She'd been shaking out the bedspread I'd yanked off the bed and when she let out her scream, it flew back over her head, temporarily blinding her. I stood there naked, dripping wet, with a lamp in my right hand, ready to bludgeon a short Guatemalan woman struggling to remove a coverlet from her head. It was absurd. She was more frightened than I was.

I covered myself with a towel and we both apologized profusely. At least I think she was apologizing; half of it was in Spanish and, as noted, my Spanish still sucks. She was happy to be shuttled out of the room and promised to come back later, although I wouldn't have blamed her it she didn't. I scooped a handful of chocolates from her cart and put the privacy sign on the door handle. Then I threw the long bolt just to make sure I didn't have another Janet Leigh/*Psycho* moment in the shower.

Replaying the last sixteen hours, it seemed insane that I would tear ass back to the hotel to save Lucy from . . . what? Worse than death? She hadn't texted or e-mailed *Help*, thank god, so what was I worried about? Maybe the break-in at my home had shaken me up more than I realized.

I dressed and went downstairs to the lobby, starting to feel like I lived there—a pretty depressing thought.

Hector was cruising the bar, keeping a watchful eye on three seniors in pastel track suits; it was a toss-up who would win if they had to go mano a mano. Amanda was hauling her gear into the corpse flower's enclosure. When she saw me she gave me a thumbs-up and sprinted over to tell me she was ninety percent sure tomorrow was the big day. I was hoping she'd be right. I cared less about the flower appearing than I did about Lucy appearing but with any luck, both would happen.

Hector joined us by the corpse flower.

"I thought you left," he said, folding his chubby hands in front of himself, eyeing Amanda and rocking back and forth.

"I came back. Is that unprecedented at Titans?"

He shook his head and wagged his finger at me. "I told you, this place is going to be happening." Amanda went back to her work and Hector stuck around to watch her climb the ladder in her snug Juicy sweatpants. He tilted his head to the right to get a better view.

"I didn't know you were such a plant lover," I said.

"Pretty little flower like that, you bet your ass. Oh, excuse me, *mamí*." I wondered if Hector had ever heard the term *jailbait*.

"Why are you so sure that Titans is going to be such a happening place this time? Bernie's had investors before, right?"

"Not like this." As he said it, he raised his chin slightly and motioned to a woman pushing through the revolving doors. She and I briefly made eye contact; I thought I recognized her.

"Who's that?"

"That's the Queen Mother," he said. I didn't get the reference.

"Shows what you know. That's Jackie Connelly, she's the grandmother of Sean Crawford."

"Very nice, is there more to it than she gets to go cootchy-coo and babysit? Wait a minute, Crawford?"

Sean Crawford was the only child of Jackie's daughter, Chantel, and the late Bobby Crawford, one of the three brothers. At the time of his death Bobby was tribal chief of the Quepochas. And his son and his widow were the only two people still officially living on the reservation.

"How can that be? Aren't there a lot of them? I mean, if they're lobbying for recognition?"

Once again, Hector was astounded by my ignorance. Amanda was gone and without her tiny butt on display alongside the corpse flower it no longer held any interest for him, so we walked to the raised lounge area near the bar. According to Hector the Quepochas had split into two factions—those supporting the Crawfords and the others aligning themselves with another family. The Crawford ranks were dwindling.

"Oksana told me the other Crawford brothers aren't allowed here anymore."

"They're not allowed on the reservation any longer either."

"Why not?"

He shrugged. "Hey, they had their turn, now it's someone else's chance to be in charge. Like the Democrats and the Republicans." I was beginning to appreciate Hector's simplified view of the world.

"They can't come here because the Mishkins got a restraining order against them. Crawfords are anti-gaming. They think if Bernie gets this loan . . ." He didn't need to finish. If Bernie got the loan he could pay off his debts and still fund the Quepochas' recognition suit. Presumably if the suit was successful and Congress officially recognized the tribe Bernie and the Crawfords would profit.

"Wouldn't they stand to make a lot of money if it happened?"

"I know," he said. "They're some crazy dudes." It was inconceivable to him that anyone would not be motivated by money. And, in truth, the amount of money being made by casinos in Connecticut was astronomical. Mother Teresa would have had a hard time turning it down.

"How crazy?" I thought of what Oksana had said about the brothers being seen at the hotel the night Lucy was to arrive.

"Crazy enough to set fire to a covered wagon on Titans property as a protest against what they called the exploitation of the tribe. They make enemies everywhere. I say live and let live, bro, you know what I mean? You know what else those crazy mo'fos did, oh, excuse me. They kidnapped a lawyer, to get her to take their case against their own tribe."

"They couldn't just call him?"

"It was a her. She was just as loco as them—she took the case. I think they call that Stockholm syndrome, or some shit like that."

I told Hector what Oksana had said about their being at the hotel, but he shook his head. "They know better than to come here when I'm around." He puffed out his chest.

"Oksana around?" I asked.

"No, and she's in trouble. She didn't show up today and she didn't even call."

Twenty-five

"Oksana's very responsible. She doesn't want to lose this job." That's what the dark-haired bartender said and she was probably right, especially if her only alternative was going back to Sergei Russianoff. So were there now two girls missing—or gone poof, to quote Stacy Winters?

I ordered a cranberry juice and club soda to make the girl stick around. Bartenders were great sources in the afternoon when there were few patrons and they had time to chat.

"Who would she have had to call," I asked, "if she was going to be out sick?"

"Mrs. Page."

Rachel Page was in charge of all of the employees at Titans. She hired, fired, and generally made life miserable for the entire staff. As Bernie's sister she was half-owner of the property—he was the face of the hotel, but she wielded considerable influence over him, especially since his wife had died.

"How did Mrs. Mishkin die?"

"Car accident. Her brakes gave out." She leaned in to elaborate. "She went over the edge on Route 293. Ugly."

I doubted there were many pretty fatal car crashes but kept that observation to myself.

"That was about six months ago, before the whole casino thing came about. She would have been so happy. She loved this place. I think she and her parents used to vacation here when she was little. She was the one who ordered that thing." The bartender chucked her chin in the direction of the corpse flower.

"Rachel wanted to cancel it, but Bernie wouldn't let her."

The corpse flower was dangerously close to the top of the enclosure. If it grew another six inches they'd have to remove the top of the enclosure and the strong smell of death would permeate the lobby.

Maybe it was time to talk to a Mishkin. I called Bernie's office. With a grunt of annoyance, his sister informed me that he was in meetings all day. When she realized I wasn't going away, she made the halfhearted suggestion that I call back in two hours—I guessed that Sveta was fully booked. I had the feeling Rachel was lying about Bernie's schedule but there was nothing I could do, so I said I'd wait. I hung up and heard the first few notes to "Für Elise," which told me I had a call coming in on my cell from someone I didn't know.

Caller ID read Shaftsbury Police Department.

"Miss Holliday?"

"Yes?"

"This is Officer Bennett of the Shaftsbury Police Department." I held my breath, waiting for him to tell me that Lucy's rental car had been found in a ditch somewhere. "Did you by any chance have too much to drink last night?"

I hadn't. Okay, maybe a small bottle of red wine from the minibar after the two drinks at the bar, but who was this guy, the party police?

"No. Why?"

"Because the car you reported stolen is currently sitting in the Titans parking lot where you said you last saw it."

I didn't have time to make up a good story—maybe I wasn't as accomplished a liar as I thought I was. "Well, it wasn't there when I called. Maybe some kids took it for a joyride and then returned it."

"Uh-huh." He didn't sound like he believed me, and I wouldn't have believed me either. We went back and forth like that for another five minutes, him chastising me for being too drunk to remember where I parked my own car and wasting the police department's time. And me, finally, meekly agreeing. I ran outside to check.

The white Subaru was the lone vehicle at the farthest end of the lot, near employee parking. That was typical of Lucy. No valet parking for her. She counted steps and took every opportunity to walk, even if she was walking toward copious amounts of high-calorie drinks.

"It makes perfect sense to me," she'd say, sucking down a guavatini. "Like diet groups have food exchanges?"

I peered inside the car and tried all the doors. There was no doubt in my mind that it was Lucy's car. We shared a fondness for chocolate mint Zone bars and Dunkin' Donuts coffee and detritus from both was in evidence. So she got here, but never made it to the front door.

Now I was officially worried and actively rooting for the Vermont ski resort scenario.

Twenty-six

Something in Stacy Winters's demeanor prepared me for a tongue-lashing. Perhaps it was the dismissive little head shake. She joined me in the Titans lobby not long after I left her another message telling her that Lucy's white Subaru had been parked in the Titans lot apparently for days. She eased into the chair opposite me and peeled the top off a well-gummed coffee cup. The look on her face told me how awful it tasted.

"I appreciate your concern for your friend, but we're a small force here and we are working on a murder investigation." She said it the way people say *I don't disagree with you,* which of course means that they do. She didn't appreciate my concern one bit.

"Yeah, how's that going?" I asked, prepared to match her barb for barb.

"We've narrowed it down to some woman or her husband." Clearly Winters wasn't going to share any information with me.

"The stolen car thing was good. Very clever." She rubbed her forehead but it did little to smooth away the deep furrows. "Show me where the car is." She took a catlike stretch getting up and she looked as tired as I felt. I'd read somewhere that with every day that passes, crimes, particularly murders, get more difficult to solve. Maybe she was feeling the pressure.

When we reached the rental car Winters produced a long metal strip and with one quick move the door popped open.

"Now I know how the bad guys do it."

"This is retro. Bad guys have master keys."

I started to lean over to go through the papers on the passenger seat and she snapped at me, "Don't touch anything."

She realized she'd scared me and held her hands out wide as if to calm me down. "And don't throw up on anything. In the unlikely event that there really is a problem here, those papers may be evidence." For the first time I was afraid that Lucy may have been in real trouble. My chest tightened, then I burst into tears.

"Pull yourself together, you're supposed to be the tough city girl, aren't you?" She almost sounded sympathetic. She called in for a team to check the car for any evidence or fingerprints, and she and I went back into the hotel. My phone rang and I scrambled to get it out, hoping once again that it would be Lucy. It was Caroline Sturgis and I let her go to voice mail.

"I take it that wasn't her." Winters flipped through her notebook. "The Russian bartender may know something about the Crawford brothers. Let's go talk to her," Winters said.

"She's not here. She didn't come in today and didn't call. I didn't want to say it before, but there have been times when Lucy hasn't called . . . when she was chasing a story or had a deadline." Winters seemed more interested now.

"Your friend is a journalist?"

"Yeah, sort of. Reality television, true crime, that sort of thing. Why?"

"Forget it. Do you have a picture of her?"

My eyes started welling up again, but I refused to let them spill over. I took a deep breath. I told her I had a few pictures of Lucy on the computer and I'd send them via e-mail.

"Don't e-mail, fax. My computer is on the blink."

Winters took off and I promised to send pictures of Lucy as soon as I could. That meant getting into Bernie Mishkin's office to use his fax machine whether he was there or not.

Twenty-seven

My plan was to e-mail a picture of Lucy to the Titans office and then have Rachel or Bernie print it out for me and fax it to the police station. It was a good plan as far as it went.

"I told you before, my brother is in meetings all day. He's not even on the premises and I'm certainly not going to let you sit at his computer and go through his e-mails." She gave a brittle laugh as if the very idea was insane.

Rachel Page would not be charmed. Or threatened. Or appealed to. Her better angels had flown off to help more responsive humans. She stood there looking as warm and fuzzy as Mrs. Danvers in *Rebecca*.

"I totally understand," I said, smiling and using my best saleswoman's voice. "I don't want to go through my own e-mails, much less someone else's. You do it. It's an e-mail from me—if I sent it, I already know what's in it, right?" I delivered this piece of logic with a jaunty smile, fully expecting a sheepish "Oh, why not." For a moment I thought she was considering, but it was just a tease.

"Out of the question," she said. Then she threw me a bone. "If you can print out your picture somewhere else I'll let you fax it from here."

Thanks. Chances are, if I could print it out somewhere else I wouldn't need to come back here to fax it. I was running out of ideas. "How about if I just hook my computer up to your printer? That way I wouldn't even accidentally see anything sensitive." Sensitive, my foot, she was probably guarding her brother's porn collection.

"You'd have to disconnect something and I couldn't allow that. I'm sorry."

Rachel Page wasn't sorry at all. She wasn't even giving a good imitation of sorry. She stood there with her arms folded, totally shut down, waiting for me to leave.

The town of Shaftsbury was about three blocks long. I'd driven past its one highway exit on my way to Titans. Shaftsbury was my best shot at an Internet café, otherwise I'd have to drive farther to Storrs and the UConn campus. I took a chance.

Shaftsbury should have been doing better. As close as it was to the casino, they'd probably expected an influx of jobs and tax dollars when the casino opened, but Shaftsbury fell just outside of the county line and there was no public transportation. If you didn't own a car it was impossible to get to the casino from there. And any tax revenues went to the state with just a pittance trickling down to the town. So Shaftsbury got the extra traffic and the guy who owned the gas station might have made a few extra bucks, but other than that, Shaftsbury got the shaft.

One-third of the stores were dotted with For Sale or For Rent signs. A large Goodwill store was there but closed for the day. In the doorway I saw a Big Y shopping cart. A bundle of rags seemed to be moving and I realized it was the homeless guy going through a paper bag filled with recent donations. For a moment I thought of stopping, but what would I have said? Remember that time we saw the dead guy? I moved on, crawling down the street looking for a computer store in a depressed area, with little chance of finding one.

Just a handful of shops were open—a laundry, a liquor store, a coffee shop, and a convenience store. Only the last showed any signs of life so I pulled into a spot right in front and went in.

The store was crammed with magazines, hair accessories, processed snack foods, cigarettes, and lottery tickets. The sales counter was fringed with them—all over the top and sides, making it look like a red and blue grass shack.

"Powerball?" the clerk asked.

I was probably the only person in the state who'd never bought a Powerball ticket, and decided to keep it that way.

"No thanks. I was looking for an Internet café." Even as I said it, it sounded ridiculous in this downtrodden town, as if I'd asked for the Jaguar dealership.

"Nothing like that here. Gotta go to Storrs, where the students are." He checked me out and must have decided I was reasonably trustworthy. "Betty's got a computer though."

"Who's that?"

According to the stack of business cards on the counter, Betty Smallwood was an attorney-at-law and a notary public. And she had an office on top of the convenience store.

"She's in. She might let you use it for a dollar or two." He pointed toward the back of the store, on the left, where a glass door was labeled with black and gold stick-on letters, B. Smallwood, Esq., Notary, Tribal Genealogist.

I climbed the too-shallow stairs up to Smallwood's third-floor office and knocked.

"Come on in."

My first view of her was of her butt, pushed in the air while she was kneeling on the floor watering her plants. She stuck a finger in the potted palm to check its moisture level before giving it any more water.

"Good idea." I said hello and she scrambled to her feet.

"I thought it was Georgie." She laughed. "From downstairs." She brushed her hands on her pants and we shook. Against the far wall were file cabinets of various colors and heights, giving it the appearance of a fake skyline, like something you'd see in an off-Broadway show. Above and on top of the cabinets were Native American memorabilia. There weren't many office machines but she had a small combo printer/scanner/fax machine similar to the one I had at home. Bingo.

I told her why I'd come and without needing a moment to think about it she cleared off a space on her desk for me to set up my laptop. My battery was running low so I needed to plug the computer in and that meant she had to find one of the overworked extension cords in the office and swap something out.

"So, you're a tribal genealogist?" I said, making small talk while she looked for something noncritical to unplug.

"Yeah. I know, everyone expects braids and lots of turquoise jewelry. I only wear it on special occasions, to please my family. Most of the time we just look like everyone else."

She might not have looked like Pocahontas that day, but she certainly didn't look like everyone else. She had thick dark hair that fell in sheets around her face and would have cost seven to eight hundred dollars for Japanese straightening if she hadn't come by it naturally. Her skin was a perfect even caramel color and it made her teeth and the whites of her eyes seem even whiter than they were.

She plugged in my computer and we sat opposite each other at her desk waiting for my computer to power up; I sent her the e-mail attachment with Lucy's photo. As it printed out she said, "So may I ask you what this is about?"

I told her about Lucy and debated whether or not to mention the Crawford brothers. As soon as I did the atmosphere in the room changed.

"Have I said something?"

"You know you did. That's why you're here, isn't it?" She was upset, thinking I'd somehow tricked her.

"I'm here because I needed a fax machine and I didn't think the Laundromat had one." Then I got it. She was the attorney the Crawford brothers had kidnapped.

Twenty-eight

"I've told this story a hundred times. My clients didn't kidnap me. I was never in any danger. My father just overreacted because he couldn't reach me for a day or two." Betty leaned back in her chair, a bemused look on her face.

"It was all a misunderstanding," she said, "but people in this area have long memories. My father in particular." She handed me Lucy's picture and the printed confirmation that the fax had been sent to the police station. Then she sat there for a while with a strange smile on her face, rolling down the sleeves of her soft plaid shirt.

Was that what *I* was doing? *Overreacting* because I couldn't reach Lucy?

"Stacy Winters is going to have a laugh when she sees where that fax came from," she said. I didn't get the joke.

Betty Smallwood represented the two surviving Crawford brothers in a number of legal matters, most significantly their dispute with the rival faction of the Quepochas tribe. I told Betty that Lucy was working on a story about Native Americans in Connecticut and gambling. I wanted her on my side so I let her think Winters was the one who'd planted the seed that the Crawford brothers might have had something to do with Lucy's disappearance.

"That woman needs to get out and find some new suspects. Every time anything goes wrong within a fifty-mile radius she wants to blame Billy and Claude. She's even tried to implicate them in Nick Vigoriti's death, which is preposterous."

"People are lining up and taking sides," she said, shaking her head. "It's as if they can smell recognition coming and they've all got their hands out. Waiting to cash in. Bobby, the oldest brother, wasn't like that."

Bobby Crawford might not have been like that, but it was understandable how some people were when individual members from recognized tribes with casinos were pulling down at least $100,000 a year and tribal leaders as much as $1.5 million a year. Just for being a member.

"It's complicated. State recognition is a start, but only federal recognition opens the door for gaming. And it's based on specific federal criteria," she said. "Membership in a tribe is simply determined by the members of that tribe."

"So if the leader enrolls you as a member, you're a member?"

"No one wants to think it happens like that, but yes, it can. Bobby used to call them the Wantabees and the Ihopesos."

Most people who claimed Native American heritage were only one-eighth or one-sixteenth. Betty herself was only one-quarter Quepochas. The Crawfords were going head-to-head with a faction of the tribe who wanted to admit hundreds of new members to get their numbers up in the hopes of solidifying their case before Congress.

"That's why they got in touch with me. Bobby Crawford was the tribal leader at the time."

"So why snatch you?" I asked. "Wasn't there a lawyer they could simply call?" I waited for her to refute my use of the word *snatch,* but she didn't.

"I was on my way back to New Haven. I hadn't spent more than four weeks on tribal lands since I'd left for college seven years earlier. I was an apple—red on the outside, white on the inside. Maybe they wanted to make a statement."

She swung around in her chair and pointed to a picture hanging on the wall behind her desk. "That's my father, Daniel Smallwood. He's the only other lawyer in Shaftsbury. He's also the leader of the rival faction."

Then again, maybe *that* was it.

"At the time I felt no more Quepochas than you probably feel . . ." She looked me up and down. "Scotch-Irish?"

"Close. Italian-Irish."

"Don't get me wrong. There weren't a lot of squaws at Yale, and if a professor wanted to give me extra points for it, I let him. My way of helping to assuage his white Anglo guilt. But I didn't play it up with a lot of fringed leather and beaded jewelry."

I believed her. She wasn't denying her heritage, it was just that she didn't think about it that much. Until the Crawfords came back into her life.

"My father was disappointed when Bobby married someone outside of the tribe. I guess he had hopes Bobby and I would one day bring the tribe together." Betty said this so unemotionally I had a hard time believing her.

"Bobby and Chantel had a child right away. No surprise, she had a bump on their wedding day. Then he died and she really *embraced the tribe,* as they say."

I bet she did. Free room and board courtesy of the Bureau of Indian Affairs and the knowledge that she and her little boy would be enrolled as members of the Quepochas tribe. And possibly a very rich member if she sided with Daniel Smallwood.

"As a licensed attorney I went before the tribal council to make the Crawfords' case. We won and the tribe agreed not to add any new members without a rigorous approval process."

"DNA testing?" I asked.

"Not that rigorous."

Betty told me they'd tried that ten years earlier and the results sent shock waves through the small community. Some leaders had less blood than they claimed, some members found out their fathers weren't their fathers, and other even more awkward bits of news surfaced, so the testing was halted and never resumed.

"Were the Crawfords ever arrested for the incident with you?"

"Arrested, but not charged. I wouldn't press charges. Without that it was purely a tribal issue. Red on red offense on tribal lands . . . the council had jurisdiction. They held a pretrial intervention on behalf of the Crawfords. We made it go away. It wasn't in anyone's interests to pursue."

On top of that, she'd come over to their side. She learned a lot about her own heritage from them. Bobby, really. He was the smart one; the other two were not as bright. Or as passionate about their cause.

The original stunt had worked. Now I wondered if the surviving brothers were dumb enough to try something similar on a nonnative off tribal lands, where it wouldn't be a tribal issue swept under the rug but a federal offense.

"Is the reservation near here?"

I tried to sound casual, but Betty Smallwood knew what I was thinking.

"They wouldn't do that."

"Why not? They shamed and charmed you into seeing their side. Maybe they thought they could do the same with a TV journalist." Lucy would have been happy to be referred to that way, although she'd be the first to admit that she cranked out low-budget reality television shows.

I waited for Betty to answer, and she searched my face trying to guess how I'd use the information.

"It's adjacent to the Titans Hotel, on the north side."

"Thank you."

We heard huffing and puffing, and the stairs creaking as they had when I climbed them. I thought it was the elderly salesclerk, then the door swung open.

"You better have some water up here." It was Detective Stacy Winters. She leaned against the doorjamb, hands low on her bony hips, and Betty pointed to a cooler near a dirty casement window.

"Where are they?" she asked.

"Papercups?"

"C'mon, let's not waste each other's time. Billy and Claude. They were seen at the hotel and as of this morning I've got physical evidence linking them to Nick Vigoriti's murder."

So now the Crawfords were officially wanted for questioning in the murder of Nick Vigoriti. My temporary status as a "person of interest"—bestowed on me by the local press, who had to say something even if it was vague and ultimately untrue—was rescinded. And if Lucy's disappearance had briefly registered on Stacy Winters's Richter scale, it had gone poof with this new evidence against her favorite suspects.

"Physical evidence, right at the scene. So I'll ask you again.

Where are they?" Winters said. It was a scene I had a feeling they'd played out before, with Betty leading in the head-to-head matchup.

"What is your problem with them? One of them not ask you to the prom or something? I don't know and I wouldn't tell you if I did. I wouldn't have to. Presumably you do know something about the law, since you're in law enforcement." Betty was in lawyer mode, but this smacked of something a tad more personal.

At a loss for words, Winters turned to me. "And what are *you* doing here?" She walked over to the watercooler, ran a finger across the top of the dusty glass jug, and decided against it. "I heard about your little escapade in Springfield last year. Some cop friend of yours called me. I hope you don't think you're going to start sticking your nose in police business up here."

Betty's crack about the prom and Winters's inability to deliver a quick comeback made me bold. "Lay back. I just came to send you the fax. It's not like there's a Kinko's in this burg." I was tempted to say, *If your office had a working computer I wouldn't be here.* I handed her the picture of Lucy that I'd just faxed to her office. She didn't even look at it—just folded it in four and stuffed it in her inside pocket.

"Okay. Mission accomplished. I got the fax."

She stood with her hands on her hips, dismissing me. Jeez, what a bitch. Part of me wanted to stick around for the cat fight, but I didn't need to be hit over the head—she wanted me gone and I was happy to oblige. I yanked out the power cord and shoved the cord and the computer in my bag. "What do I owe you for letting me use the computer, Ms. Smallwood?"

"Forget it."

I made my way down the stairs, nearly bumping into Georgie, who'd crept up to eavesdrop. "You might want to let them talk for a bit," I said, trying to spare him.

"Is it about Billy and Claude?" he whispered, walking back down the stairs. "She don't like them."

I nodded. "Does everyone know about them?" I asked.

"I know everybody. They all come in to buy the Powerball tickets. I can tell who's having fun and who's desperate." He fell just short of telling me what he meant by that. "You're not a cop, too, are you?"

"Me? I'm a gardener." That got me a smile but no more information from Georgie. I didn't want to be around when Winters and Betty finished up, so I kept walking, to the front of the store, where I handed Georgie a dollar for a bottle of water. Across the street I saw the Big Y shopping cart and the walking bundle of rags.

"You know that guy?" I asked, cracking open the bottle and taking a long pull.

"Sure. He'll be in later. I let him use the facilities—they don't let him hang around the gas station no more; owner says he scares people away," Georgie said. "I think it's the owner scares them away."

"Give him this, okay?" I handed Georgie a twenty and walked out to my car.

I had the sinking feeling that Lucy was mixed up in all of this—it had two handsome guys *and* a good story. I drove back to Titans trying to figure out what to do next. Just before the turnoff into the Titans lot was a hidden driveway I hadn't noticed before and a small handwritten sign: PROPERTY OF QUEPOCHAS, STAY THE HELL OUT.

I didn't.

Twenty-nine

In the early seventeenth century, well before it was a state, the Connecticut colony gave the Quepochas 17,000 acres of prime farmland. Who knows why? Guilt over killing so many of them with guns or disease? Fear that they would encroach on lands inhabited by European settlers? Whatever the reason, there was an acknowledgment of their existence even before the Revolutionary War. And an attempt was made to live amicably with them. Over the years, members moved off or assimilated. Large tracts of tribal lands were sold by tribal leaders until the reservation reached its present size of approximately 300 acres—small for a reservation but huge for a property in Connecticut.

For some lucky tribes, the reservation is a tax-free gated community where few people work, but that's by choice. Why work when the money from gaming just keeps falling on your head? Other tribes suffer from as much as eighty-five percent unemployment—and that's not because the members are staying in their mansions, eating bonbons.

The Quepochas reservation was neither. From what I could see, most of the reservation's inhabitants seemed to be dead, as evidenced by the lack of homes and the dozens of listing, wafer-thin tombstones I passed driving the dirt road that ran through the property.

Betty Smallwood had told me that enrolled members of the tribe were not required to live on the reservation. Hell, most of them got away as soon as they could, and as far away as possible. Like Betty herself had done.

Unofficially, a handful did live there, scattered across the reservation, scratching out an existence in shacks and cabins and quietly dying out. Officially, it was just Chantel and Sean in a two-room cinder-block house close to the road.

The farther I drove the more the road narrowed and the potholes deepened. It reminded me of the road to Oksana's place; she was on a reservation, too, in a way. The switchbacks took me higher and although I hadn't noticed it on the way up, on one side of the mountain I could now see the top of Titans. There were fewer tombstones and still no houses, just the occasional dilapidated shack built into the side of the mountain. I pulled over to a carved-out spot on the road to enjoy the view.

Peak time was probably in the fall when the mountain would be awash in color, but it looked pretty good to me; I fished out my phone to take a picture.

Just then it rang.

"Where the hell have you been?" the woman asked.

It was Lucy.

She'd been trying to reach me for the past three days. When she called the hotel, I had checked out. When she tried me at home, I'd already left to come back to Titans. And the cell didn't work until I drove up the mountain and got a signal.

"Where the hell are *you*?" I asked.

"Well, I'm not one hundred percent sure."

"Can you talk? Are you safe?"

"Yes. I'm alone now. I don't know when they'll be back. Come get me."

Thirty

Before Lucy and I were to meet at Titans, she'd had an appointment. With Billy and Claude Crawford. They were her sources for an exposé on casino gambling that involved some of the most prominent names in this part of the state and some pretty unsavory characters as well. The three of them had met in the parking lot outside of Titans. I watched the sun go down as she told me what happened.

"Didn't your mother ever tell you not to get into a car with two strange men?" I asked.

"I don't remember the stuff my mother told me. Besides, I didn't get in a car with two men; Billy had to meet someone in the hotel; he joined us later." Lucy and Claude drove to the Crawfords' attorney to discuss what they knew and how best to reveal it.

"You went to Betty Smallwood's?" I asked, incredulous.

"You know her?" Now it was Lucy's turn to be surprised.

"I just came from her office. I showed her a picture of you and she didn't bat an eyelash. She didn't utter a word about having met you." That was one cool customer.

"After I left the message for you I called this other guy I was supposed to meet," she said.

"Nick Vigoriti?"

"How do you know this?" she asked, exasperated that I was cutting into her story.

"*I* met him instead." Now I understood some of Nick's cryptic remarks. He had thought I was Lucy, in the hotel to interview him for the casino story. And so, obviously, did some other people who had showed an inordinate amount of interest in a woman who was there to write about the corpse flower. I told her Nick was dead but she already knew.

"Betty called Claude and told him. That's why the guys haven't wanted to drive back. Some local cop has a real hard-on for them and probably thinks they did it. The boys stashed their car in the woods and we walked the rest of the way here."

"And where is here?"

She was somewhere on the reservation in a log cabin off a dirt road. "It's kind of nice, like one of those places pictured in the Sunday *Times* real estate section with a view that you can never afford. High on the mountain, lake, there's even a small waterfall in the distance."

Waterfront property notwithstanding, she was brought to a secret place, car stashed, and incommunicado for three days. Any minute she'd start speaking Swedish. I forced myself to stay calm and not scream at her.

"Okay, why are you still there?" There was a silence and after being Lucy's friend for many years and through many relationships I knew exactly what it meant.

"Jeez, Lucy, *both* of them?"

"No, just Claude. You have to see him, he's gorgeous. He's got this amazing hair and skin. Our kids would be phenomenal."

Oh, brother. The only reservation in Lucy's future was at Balthazar, downtown, table by the window, but she was playing out some fantasy. One of us had to be the grown-up.

"It's not as if I just met him," she rationalized. "We've been e-mailing for weeks—I felt as if I knew him." I tried not to be judgmental with friends, but my silence smacked of disapproval.

"Lucy, I just heard the cops say they had evidence that implicated the Crawfords in Nick's death. What do you know about that?"

"I know they've been persecuted by some psycho local cop with an ax to grind . . ."

"And hotel security at Titans has instructions not to admit the Crawfords," I said. "There's a restraining order against them entering the hotel, so Billy's got to be lying about meeting someone there. Luce, physical evidence. Ted Bundy was cute, too. Not my type, but someone thought he was cute."

I checked my watch; it would be dark in about thirty minutes, and it was getting chilly. As it was, I didn't know if I could make it back down the mountain in the dark with all of those switchbacks—and the very real possibility of going over the side like poor Mrs. Mishkin made it an unattractive prospect. I had to find her, and soon.

The light was fading but I had a picture of the spot on my phone and Lucy had given me a description of what she could see from the cabin; I tried to match it up with what I saw from my perch on the side of the dirt road. She told me the lake was on her right.

"That's west," I said.

"Is it? Oh yeah, setting sun." Clearly she hadn't been a Girl

Scout. Neither had I for that matter—west was the Henry Hudson Parkway and east was the FDR, what else did you need to know in Manhattan?

"I've got it!" she said. When Lucy rented the car, YoDrive had provided her with a TomTom, a portable global positioning system. Since no New Yorker leaves anything of any value in her car, she had automatically taken it with her. She rummaged through her bag to get the Tom.

"Great! What does it say?"

She waited for a satellite signal. Finally the screen lit up. "It says I'm screwed. I'm at the corner of nowhere and battery low," she said, frustrated. "I'm a speck. What's the point of this thing? You have to know where you are to know where you are."

I told her to minimize the screen to see as much of the surrounding area as possible. She was somewhere west of 95, which was not much help since so was most of the United States.

"Plug in Titans as a destination," I said. If she'd used it on the drive up it would have been her last address on the TomTom. She groaned.

"I didn't use it. The clerk at YoDrive said all I had to do was take 95, so that's what I did."

"It's near Academy Road. Start with that."

Titans's exact address was on my Jeep's system and I ran to get it before the power drained on Lucy's Tom. We waited until her handheld unit processed the information. She was eleven miles from Titans, but the TomTom was having a rough time choosing a route selection since there weren't any established roads through the reservation.

"Keep at it," I said, "and call me back if something comes up. Wait a minute, give me your longitude and latitude. Maybe I can figure out how to use that to find you."

"How do I do that?"

I told her to hit browse map but it was too late. The TomTom ran out of power.

"Lucy, is there electricity in that cabin?"

"No."

"Well, light some candles and make a fire. And save your cell power. Turn it back on in one hour. I'll call you to let you know where I am." *Assuming I knew.*

Before I risked losing my cell signal, I made one more call.

"Paradise Diner."

Babe and company were gearing up for the dinner crowd, not as busy as breakfast or lunch, but busy enough so that Babe didn't answer the phone herself.

"She's with some customers. Want me to get her?" Alba, the budding rock singer/waitress, took a message. I could hear her making change at the register, and she read the message back to me with no reaction at all to its contents: *Lucy missing, searching Quepochas reservation, just in case you never see me again. Paula.*

"Okay, so, like, is that it?"

"That's it."

Thirty-one

A former colleague once dragged me to a foreign film called *The Wages of Fear*, starring Yves Montand, a French hottie from the fifties. The movie was about a couple of guys who were so broke they agreed to drive a truck filled with nitroglycerin across the proverbial hundred miles of bad road. Most of the film showed a nervous, white-knuckled driver and a wild-eyed passenger stopping and starting the car while they navigated the treacherous road.

All I needed was the passenger.

Farther on from the spot where I'd spoken to Lucy, the road had fewer switchbacks, but other than that, it was really only good for mountain goats or Dall sheep. The kind you see in *National Geographic* magazines and wonder how the hell it is they don't fall off the side of a craggy bluff. Luckily the Jeep is the automotive equivalent of a mountain goat. All of those car commercials that are so obviously Photoshopped to show cars at the tops of arches and hoodoos in Colorado or Utah actually have some basis in reality.

As long as I kept to a snail's pace, I made progress. The road had to have been at a forty-five-degree angle in some spots and even more in others with only intermittent stretches where I could kick butt and drive a whopping eight or ten miles an hour.

Even with my brights on I could only see about twenty feet ahead of the car. Without another vehicle in front of me as a frame of reference, the road seemed to get narrower, at times seeming just inches wider than the Jeep. Branches scraped both sides of the car. I pulled left to avoid them on the right and a stubby shrub reached in and left a long scratch on my cheek, scaring the hell out of me. Then I overcompensated and hugged the mountain so closely on the next turn that I smacked in the passenger-side window. The sound startled me and I stopped to survey the damage. To the car and to my face.

I slid out of the car, clinging first to the door, then the hood. In the headlights I saw hundreds or maybe thousands of gnats or midges, so dense they looked like mist rising from the ground. I brushed them from my arms and flicked them away from my face and hair. I inched around to the passenger side and saw the mirror hanging by a shred of plastic. I tried to snap it off, but one thick plastic-coated wire wouldn't give up the ghost. I held the mirror and looked at my distorted reflection. There was a long pink line on my face that was puffing up but no blood. I convinced myself the image was magnified and the scratch wasn't really as long as it appeared.

The bugs were getting to me so I hustled back to the driver's side of the car, stumbling on a few loose rocks. I remembered reading somewhere that small rocks gouged out of a road or hiking trail were frequently evidence of bears looking for food. Oh, good. Another thing to worry about. I climbed back into the driver's seat, and continued creeping uphill for almost another hour.

The mountain flattened out a bit after the next two sets of switchbacks and I had my fingers crossed that I could get past them before the sun went down completely. I unconsciously leaned in with every turn as if that would make a serious aerodynamic difference inside a two-ton vehicle. I was so intent on reaching the mesa I forgot my promise to call Lucy and didn't do it until reaching the relative safety of a clearing just short of the top.

Until I stopped driving and got out of the car I hadn't realized how tightly I was gripping the steering wheel; when I released it the tension drained from my neck and shoulders.

Just to be on the safe side, I reached back into the car to put on the emergency brake; that's when I noticed the odometer read 24,507—I'd only gone six miles. I speed-dialed Lucy's number but there was no answer—she must have still had the phone turned off; I'd check back in fifteen or twenty minutes.

I hadn't eaten anything all day and was starting to feel it. I never kept food in the car, other than the occasional Zone bar, and I checked the storage box between the driver's and passenger's seats to see if I'd get lucky.

Bingo. Chocolate mint. Okay, it was a little hard, but it was better than nothing. I walked to the back of the car and opened the hatch. The case of bottled water I usually had stashed in the car was covered by the tarp and garden tools that had shifted in the course of my climb up the mountain. I moved the tarp, the pitchfork, and some hand tools and cracked open a bottle of water. I sat in the back dangling my legs and looking at the stars.

High on the mountain, I thought I saw a light. Hopefully it was Lucy in the Crawfords' cabin. Then I looked down at the long slow climb that I'd just made, and saw something else—two specks of light. Moving slowly, but definitely moving. Judging by how long it had taken me, it would take whoever it was at least an hour to get to me, so that gave me an hour to get to Lucy.

But I had a bigger problem. First there was the overpowering smell. It was a steaming pile of fresh scat. Which is a nice way of saying bear shit. Then there was the long low growl.

Thirty-two

When you're hiking in black bear country and confront a bear, half the guidebooks tell you to drop into a fetal position and cover your head. The other half tell you to wave your arms like a lunatic and make noise—some parks even sell bear bells that you're supposed to jingle to make the bears go away. This struck me as contradictory advice and I had about three seconds to decide which to follow—but I'm not a fetal position kind of gal.

What the guidebooks never tell you to do is throw a Zone bar and a cell phone at the bear, but that's what I did. It wasn't intentional, it was a reflex—they just flew out of my hands. I remembered the bit about making noise and reached into the Jeep, grabbing two hand weeders and furiously clanking the tines together. Then I thought, *Just get in the freaking car!*

The same reflex as before made me fling the weeders in the bear's general direction and jump in the car, closing the hatch from inside. I scrambled to the driver's seat and raised the windows as fast as I could. The black bear is generally harmless and would really prefer eating berries or garbage to human flesh, but when you're on foot and so is he—despite the fact that it's a different animal and you're on a different continent—visions of King Kong pop into your head and that, inevitably, makes you the screaming, writhing Fay Wray.

I had the presence of mind to lock the doors and was catching my breath when the bear lumbered over, stood on his hind legs, and put his front paws on the driver's side of the car. In the bear's mouth was the Zone bar, the wrapper sticking to his teeth. He didn't mind that it was stale. He seemed to like it, even the paper. In his paw was my cell phone, which must have looked like just another hunk of chocolate to him because that was what he ate next.

The bear took his sweet time walking in front of the car, swatting at the gnats, turning over rocks looking for fat juicy bugs, and finally lumbering off into the night. When I lost him in the headlights it was the first time in hours I was glad I couldn't see that far ahead of me.

Now I had no food and no phone. Lucy didn't know where I was and I didn't know if her hosts, the Crawfords, had returned. The two specks of light I'd seen below had disappeared, probably struggling to negotiate one of the switchbacks, but whoever it was he was getting closer and closer the longer I sat there, so I put the car into drive and took off again.

There was a surprisingly flat stretch of road ahead of me; still I was careful not to get too cocky just in case there was a sheer drop or a second bear on the other side.

The flickering lights above me grew bigger. That was either good news or not; by this time, every tree stump was a bear, every screeching owl was an assailant, and I still didn't know what I'd find at the cabin.

I put the radio on for background noise and that's just what it was, all static. I neurotically went around the dial twice as if that was going to improve the reception. Then I remembered AM. I switched frequencies and got a little buzz, then an oldies station. It was better than nothing and helped keep my mind off lions, tigers, bears, and whoever was in the car behind me. Half an hour later I was listening to Freda Payne singing about her unfortunate wedding night. I was mouthing the words when the road simply ended. No more turns, no more switchbacks, no more nothing. Just the hint of a footpath between the trees.

I stopped the car, opened the moon roof, and stood up on the driver's seat, trying to get my bearings and find the flickering lights I'd seen before. There they were. And this time I could see the faint outline of a cabin.

I climbed into the backseat to look for anything that might be useful. The battery in the lantern was dead. I had a tarp, a few bungee cords, and a pitchfork. I had no idea what I was going to do with them, but I wanted to feel prepared, so I took them just in case.

The folded tarp fit under my arm, I wrapped the bungee cords around my waist, and I carried the pitchfork in my right hand, using it to hold back branches as I made my way through the brush to the cabin. There was a small clearing in front of it, but the cabin was carved into the side of the mountain, Anasazi style; without any lights on it would have been nearly impossible to see. I crept closer to the door, desperate to hear any sounds inside. Nothing. I rapped on the door with the pitchfork.

"Don't . . . don't come any closer," yelled a shaky voice from inside. "I have a gun."

"Lucy, it's me, Paula." I took a deep breath and straightened up from my fighting stance.

"Thank god," she said, opening the door, white as a ghost.

She had an iron fire poker in her hand and if it hadn't been me, she would have been prepared to use it. I had the pitchfork. We looked like a couple of settlers about to go at it.

"That's not a gun."

"What was I supposed to say, 'I have a poker'? And what is that," she asked, looking at the pitchfork, "a house gift?" Her color came back and so did her smart mouth. Neither of us wanted to admit we'd been scared.

"Mother told me never to go visiting empty-handed," I said, hugging her.

She squeezed back, then pulled away, smacking me on the shoulder. "You didn't call me."

"A bear ate my phone," I said, tossing the pitchfork and tarp on the table. I don't think she believed me.

The cabin was two rooms with a packed-dirt floor, rough-hewn cabinets, a wooden table and chairs in one room, and two monastic beds in the other. One window was carved out of the mud that was the front of the structure.

"I like what you've done with the place. So where are you and Claude going to register? Tuba City Trading Post?"

"Shut up. You caught me at a weak moment, I was very vulnerable. You're right, it was crazy. Now, can you please get us out of here?"

Good question. We could make it to the car, but I didn't love that drive in the daylight going forward, I'd probably hate it at night going backward until there was a spot wide enough for me to turn around in.

"Is there a flashlight here?" I asked.

"No. There weren't exactly a lot of cabinets to check. I bet when these guys misplace something they don't have to look for it for very long."

I went into the other room to search under the beds for any boxes where tools or supplies might be stashed, but no luck. Lucy ran in a few minutes later.

"Paula . . ." she whispered. "I hear something. What's that?" Lucy grabbed hold of my hand and squeezed so tightly my fingers went numb. I closed my eyes to shut out everything else. Apart from the pounding of my own heart, I heard something, too.

Whoever it was would be able to get in; all we had going for us was the element of surprise. We shoved the heavy table closer to the door and rearranged the chairs; I planned to use one of them as a weapon, if necessary. If it was someone familiar with the cabin, tripping over the furniture would slow them down and give us some time. I unwrapped the bungee cords from around my waist, criss-crossed them at ankle height three feet inside the door, and stretched them from the cabinet legs to one of the beds and from the chairs to the other bed so that in the dark, anyone entering would think he was okay and then be tripped up a few steps inside. It would buy us a few minutes at best. I told Lucy to line up our arsenal—the pitchfork, the poker, a chair, and the tarp.

"That's it?" I asked. "No big frying pan à la Wile E. Coyote?"

"I guess the boys don't cook much, they certainly didn't offer me anything. I haven't eaten for hours and you know how cranky I get. I was kinda hoping for those big Navajo pancakes like you get outside of Vegas."

"I know where you can get some of those," I said. "Keep it down."

She chattered quietly about Claude and about her stay, just to keep herself calm, almost like a mother soothing a baby, all the while the cracking of twigs and muttering of voices grew louder.

I told Lucy to find some matches, then kill all the candles and the lanterns except for one. "And get your poker. You may need it."

Thirty-three

The faint rumble outside grew louder. Lucy was hyperventilating. She stood up and held the poker like a golf club with instructions from me to aim at the knees, shins, or forearms—a cute cop in Virginia had once told me those were the best places to go for. Minimal strength required, maximum damage inflicted.

The door creaked open and we stood flattened against the wall behind it. In seconds, as I hoped, bodies tumbled over the bungee cords; in the dark I couldn't tell how many. I threw the tarp over them and Lucy started maniacally flailing away to a chorus of screams and "what the . . ." A figure in skintight jeans stood in the doorway, taking off a helmet and shaking out her hair. Babe Chinnery.

"Stop, stop." I pulled Lucy back before she killed somebody and three unhappy men scrambled to their feet.

"How did you get here? I would have sworn you weren't even going to get my message," I said.

"Alba's a good kid. She said you sounded *funny,* which at her age could mean anything from indigestion to an oncoming freight train. Then I remembered seeing you tear out of Springfield yesterday looking like the devil was chasing you, so I thought maybe something was up. Luckily Charlie, Danny, and Ken were in the diner when you called."

They had been heading back to Marcus Dairy to pick up Danny's bike. Since men don't usually say no to Babe, she had had her choice among three Harleys and she got them to take her to the reservation and then climb the mountain.

"I'd just gotten my turkey and cranberry wrap," Danny said, rubbing the life back into the thigh that Lucy had whacked. "It's probably all soggy by now."

"You have food?" Lucy asked, sidling up to him.

"You gotta be kidding. First you crack me in the leg with a poker and then you expect me to give you my dinner?"

"Some people might consider it foreplay."

"Ooooh, I like this girl. C'mon outside, honey, dinner is served."

"You're lucky Caroline Sturgis isn't here, too," Babe said, following Danny and Lucy out to the bikes.

That stopped me in my tracks. "Are you serious?"

"She's been camped out at the diner for thirty-six hours with some news she's itching to tell you," Babe said. "She needs to get out and have more fun . . . like you girls."

Oh, yeah, this was big fun.

"The ride was sweet," Danny said, climbing onto his bike with Lucy wrapping herself around him. "Until we met those a-holes."

"What a-holes?" I asked.

"Some big guy and a runt trying to get up the mountain in a

crappy Toyota," Danny said. "They had a hell of a blowout. Looked like they drove over a steel claw."

"Hey, we told them we'd help them out on our way back, but they got rude, yelling in some foreign language. They left their car on the road, and started back down the hill, smacking each other and taking turns swigging from a bottle of vodka."

Thirty-four

The six of us made our way back to my car. With Charlie's help I backed the Jeep down to a spot where I could safely turn it around.

The Ukrainians' car had to be moved out of the way so the Jeep could pass. They'd left the windows open and the doors weren't locked, but they hadn't been so accommodating as to leave the key in the ignition.

With five hundred or so pounds among them, not including leathers, Charlie and the other guys tried moving the car with brute force but it wouldn't budge. They tried again and when the veins started popping out on necks and foreheads we made them stop. They looked at one another and I heard Danny say, under his breath, "Dude, I know she's hot, but I'm not scratching up my bike to move that hunk of junk."

The assembled brain trust gave it some thought, but pushing the car with either the Jeep or the bikes was not a good plan. Besides, we might overdo it and send the car sailing off the side of the mountain. In any event, it wasn't necessary. Babe Chinnery climbed off Charlie's bike and brushed the three men aside. She slid into the Toyota and her head disappeared under the steering wheel.

"Six years of hanging out with drunken roadies and musicians who frequently lost their wallets, their airline tickets, their wives . . . and their car keys," she explained, calmly hot-wiring the car. Another of her not-so-hidden talents. Once the engine came to life, Charlie put the car in neutral and single-handedly pushed it into the brush and out of the way into one of the wider switchbacks. Macho man stuff, undoubtedly for Babe's benefit.

The Toyota was a junker—its owner was clearly not the kind of guy who took his car in for a tune-up when the little red light flashed and told him to. Red masking tape held one of the brake light covers on. Inside, the car stank of cigarette smoke; fast-food wrappers littered the floor of the backseat; and there were plenty of beer cans, as well as three empty bottles of Popov vodka.

"Nothing but the best," Babe said. "You know these losers?"

"Not in the biblical sense," I said.

One of my hand weeders was embedded in the Toyota's left front tire and I poked around in the dirt road as much as I could by the headlights of the Harleys looking for the other one—I didn't want any of us to suffer the same fate the Michelin Man and his friend had.

"Find it?" Babe asked.

"No. Just didn't want to take any chances." A ridiculous thing to say under the circumstances.

"I think this Toyota was the car I saw on the way to Oksana's. The same one that followed me to the gas station on the highway," I said.

"What the hell for?" Babe asked.

Lucy was hovering, wolfing down Danny's soggy but still

edible turkey sandwich. Danny stood by, wondering how she'd thank him.

"Why are you looking at me?" she said, mouth full.

"They were following me because they thought I was you."

Lucy was used to being followed, at parties, at conferences; she'd even been followed into the ladies' room once at a bar on the Upper East Side, but that time it hadn't been entirely unexpected or unwelcome.

"Why would anyone want to follow me?"

"It has to be your story."

"The Quepochas' fight for recognition has been going on for twenty years," Lucy said. "And people have been arguing about casinos for just as long."

Maybe. But Titans's financial difficulties had only recently come to light. I was betting that they were connected and that connection was the catalyst for Nick's murder.

The bikers helped me load my gear and tools on top so that Babe and Lucy could ride with me. Once again the blue tarp and the bungee cords came in handy. In the car I brought the girls up to speed, as Charlie slowly led us down the mountain. They left us at the entrance to Titans with a standing invitation for a meal on the house at the Paradise; Lucy promised Danny a personal, gourmet thank-you in New York in exchange for his turkey sandwich.

I suggested we crash in my room and drive home in the morning. "There are two double beds and a love seat. Does that work for you two?" Babe and Lucy agreed and we walked to Lucy's rental car to get her overnight bag. Even from a distance we could tell something was wrong. The trunk of the car wasn't closed properly. Inside it, Lucy's expensive red leather suitcase was zipped closed but with a small scrap of fabric stuck in the teeth.

"Hey, that's my Burberry." She unzipped the bag and saw that her usually carefully packed clothing had been rummaged and thoughtlessly restuffed in the bag, her expensive scarf stuck in the zipper.

"You know, I'm used to this when I fly," she said, pissed off and checking to see if anything was missing. "Generally there's a slip of paper explaining why it's critical to national security for some lonely TSA guy to sniff my undies, but *here,* for crying out loud?"

"It was probably the cops," I said. "I reported you as missing." I'd call Winters in the morning to tell her everything was all right.

"You did? That was so sweet," she said, refolding her things.

"Don't get too mushy," I said. "No one paid any attention until I reported your *car* as stolen."

"Nevertheless," she said, "you're a real *friend.*"

So was Babe. If it hadn't been for her, Lucy and I would still be on the mountain with two angry Ukrainians trudging up to meet us. Maybe I wasn't quite as alone in the world as I sometimes felt. And maybe I shouldn't keep quite so tight a grip on that *F* word.

A handful of stragglers were hanging out in the Titans lobby when we entered. Hector chatted with a young Hispanic couple near the corpse flower and gave me a nod as I came in, then a longer look when he saw Babe and Lucy trailing behind me. On our way to the elevator, Helayne, the bartender, waved. I knew she wanted me to go over, but I pretended it was just a hello wave; I'd had as much excitement and new information as I could handle for one night.

"What, is this your new hangout?" Lucy asked. "Does everyone here know you?"

"It's your fault. I've spent so much time in this lobby waiting for you, I was beginning to feel like an employee . . . or a hooker."

In the room we dumped our things and I put on the television for white noise. Lucy took the love seat, Babe and I the double beds. Before long we'd spread out and had Hoovered the contents of the minibar; we sat in our underwear drinking little nips as if it was a pajama party.

"How did you ever get mixed up with these guys?" Babe asked.

"The Titans casino is never going to happen," Lucy said, popping peanut M&M's into the air and catching them in her mouth. "At least that's my story. The Crawford brothers don't want the casino," she said, searching for the last nut in the bag. They'd seen what had happened on other reservations when the casino operators came in. A handful of tribal leaders got fabulously wealthy, and the majority of the members—if they really were members—got stipends, which turned the young people into drug addicts and wastrels—chronically unemployed, undereducated, and more interested in flashy cars and electronics than in preserving their culture.

"That may be honorable, but is it really up to them if that's what most of the tribe wants?" I asked.

"According to them, they *are* most of the tribe, one of the seven original families of record in the 1910 census, at least legitimate ones—although Daniel Smallwood has been quietly recruiting members for the last few years with the promise of a big casino payoff," Lucy said. "The newest legitimate member of the tribe is their nephew, the famous baby Sean."

When Lucy agreed to meet with the Crawfords, they had suggested she also get in touch with their old friend Nick Vigoriti. They knew the tribal side of the story and Nick knew the hotel side.

"What did *he* have against the casino?" Babe asked.

Lucy shook her head. "I never found out," she said, crumpling the M&M bag.

Just then, in the same way that your eyes eventually get used to the dark and you can make out things you couldn't moments earlier, the white noise of the television turned into real words, "Breaking News."

Detective Stacy Winters spoke. Claude Crawford had been apprehended near the old Yankee Shoe factory. *William James Crawford is a fugitive but we have good information and feel that he will be in custody soon. The two brothers are believed to have been responsible for the recent murder of Nicholas Anthony Vigoriti. Anyone with information on the whereabouts of William Crawford is urged to dial the number on your screen.*

The reporter went on to chronicle the brothers' past offenses, including the covered wagon fire. File footage showed the blaze and two staggeringly handsome men being led away. "Now I know why you stayed," Babe said.

"And now you know why he didn't come back," I said.

"How can they say this stuff without being sure?" Babe said. She knew how; we all did. And being even a small part of the system, Lucy felt rotten about it.

"You met him," Babe said. "Did he seem like a killer to you?"

Lucy didn't think so, but she had been so taken with Claude that she hadn't paid much attention to Billy.

"He was younger than Claude. He had a Michael's shopping bag with him."

"Does that make him a nice guy?"

"No! But it made him look . . . I don't know, craft-y . . . safe, normal," she said.

Unless there was a gun in the bag, I thought. I could tell Babe was thinking the same thing.

Four loud knocks on the door jolted us. Lucy yelped; Babe jumped up and ran for her handbag.

"Do criminals knock?" Lucy whispered.

Sometimes. If they don't want you to think they're criminals. "Who is it?" I asked, trying to sound tough.

"It's Hector, ma'am. And the police."

Thirty-five

Lucy and I asked for a few minutes to dress.

"Hector, we have to stop meeting like this," I said, opening the door. The roly-poly security guard was flanked by the same two cops who'd found Lucy's car in the parking lot.

"One of you ladies Lucinda Cavanaugh?"

Lucy raised her hand shyly as if she was in school; that was probably the last time anyone had called her Lucinda.

The two cops were following up on an anonymous report of a woman stranded in a cabin on the Quepochas reservation. We all looked at Lucy to see what she'd say; it took her all of thirty seconds to get her story together.

"I *was* stranded, briefly, but my friends came and gave me a lift home." That was one way to put it—I was a novice liar compared to Lucy.

"Ms. Cavanaugh, you do know that that domicile has been

used as a hiding place for William and Claude Crawford, who are wanted for questioning in the murder of Nick Vigoriti?"

"I don't know anything about that. No one was there when I arrived." Which was technically true at the time. "I was hiking and I ran out of trail mix so I got tired. The cabin seemed like a good place to wait it out until my friends could come to get me." Now she was pushing it. I wished I could tell her to keep it simple.

"You were hiking on the Quepochas reservation? Ms. Cavanaugh, we have information that suggests you were brought to that cabin against your will."

"Absolutely not. Who knew you weren't supposed to hike there? I thought it was part of the Appalachian Trail." Even Hector snorted at that one. "My friends will tell you what a health nut I am. I'd had a long drive from New York City and simply wanted to stretch my legs." If Lucy didn't watch it, she'd tick these guys off and finish telling her story at the police station. Strangely enough, they seemed to believe her.

"It's true," I said. "She's a walker. She even counts steps." The exchange was surreal.

Babe said nothing. She stood in her underwear and a Rush T-shirt, with her arms folded, looking tough. The cops seemed to know they weren't going to get anything out of her, but they tried anyway. She gave one-word answers that were vague enough to be useless. And Lucy and I had branded ourselves as flakes—first, me by reporting Lucy's car as stolen when it was right there in the Titans parking lot, and now Lucy for having gone walkabout on a strange trail with only a bag of gorp in her back pocket.

If Lucy didn't tell the cops that Claude took her to the cabin, he couldn't be charged with abducting her; that would solve at least one of his legal problems. Like Betty had, Lucy helped Claude dodge a big bullet.

Just then, the elevator bell rang and I heard voices in the hall. One of them I recognized as Stacy Winters's. She was yakking on a cell phone and hung up just as she got to my room.

"What do we have here? Have you girls been grilling cheese sandwiches on the hotel radiator? No, it's something else, isn't it?"

We all waited for her routine to finish, then one of the uniformed cops spoke up.

"This is Ms. Cavanaugh," he said, pointing to Lucy. "She has assured us that she's all right and in fact went to the Crawfords' cabin alone and of her own volition."

"So, you weren't abducted, not missing, just *out*." She resisted the urge to use the word *poof*.

"That's correct," Lucy said. Babe's example and her own successful exchange with the two less experienced cops gave her the confidence to stand up to Winters. "I'm quite all right. Although I'm a little put out that your men felt the need to go through the bag in the trunk of my car."

"Yeah, yeah," Winters said. "If you want to make a claim for damages it's form C104. You can download it from the town's Web site. Ms. Holliday, I think the sooner you and your friends leave our little town, the happier we'll all be. You ladies have a good night."

When she was a safe distance away, Babe mouthed the word *bitch*. I agreed.

Thirty-six

After a full two hours of sleep, I woke up at 6 A.M. Through half-open eyes I saw Babe fully dressed and holding a cup of coffee.

"You didn't make that in the room, did you?" I'd heard horror stories that they used the same brush to clean the coffeepot as they used to clean the toilet.

"Not a chance. Got it downstairs. There's a very chatty waitress named Laurie in the coffee shop. She thinks both brothers were in on it and were trying to use Lucy as their alibi." We looked at Lucy, curled up, still asleep on the love seat. "The bell-boy disagrees. I haven't had a chance to poll the rest of the staff."

"*¿Quién sabe?*" I said.

Now that Claude was in jail, I knew Lucy would want to see him, at least to say goodbye, so I suggested Babe take the Jeep back to Springfield. Lucy and I would drive back later in the day and I'd pick up my car at the diner.

"You sure?"

"Are you kidding? You saved our asses last night."

I got up, found my bag, and fished around for my car keys. Babe rooted around in her bag, too.

"What are you looking for, a cell?"

"I'll give you a cell phone, too. Here, take mine. I have Neil's cell at home—if you need to reach me just speed-dial number 1." She gave me her phone and I shoved it in my pocket.

"This may come in handier." She handed me something in a leopard-print case. It was Thomas A. Swift's Electric Rifle, better known as a Taser, model number C2.

"Take it. You never know."

Thirty-seven

The idea of zapping someone with a Taser made me so nervous, I didn't even want to hold the damn thing. But I thought back to the previous night, planning to defend myself with a pitchfork and a tarp like some horticultural gladiator, and I relented. I let Babe show me how to use it.

The Taser Babe owned was a non–law enforcement, consumer model and fired two small electrodes that would work as far as fifteen feet away from the intended target. After firing its one charge, it could also be used as a direct contact stun gun that could penetrate up to two inches of clothing.

"You couldn't kill someone with this, could you?"

"Oh, you mean like a pitchfork?" She had a point. You could kill someone with virtually anything, but under normal circumstances the Taser wasn't lethal. It sent a charge to the target's central nervous system, temporarily incapacitating him. She handed me two cartridges.

"Just in case," she said. "But once should be enough. Don't get crazy. And then run like hell. Don't hang around admiring your handiwork." I didn't ask how she'd developed this strategy and whether she'd ever had occasion to use it, but now I knew why she wasn't afraid to be alone in the diner at night.

I left a note for the still sleeping Lucy and walked Babe out to the Jeep, which was practically hidden by a deluxe coach parked diagonally in four spaces. Maybe business was picking up at Titans.

"If you're not back by tonight," Babe said, "I'm calling the cops, do you read me?" I promised to check in in a few hours if Lucy and I weren't going to make it home by the time Babe closed the diner.

Babe drove off and I headed back into the hotel for my first caffeine fix of the day. Laurie in the Titans coffee shop was alone, reading the paper at the counter.

"Looks like they caught those boys."

"Looks like," I said. I glanced at the paper over her shoulder for a while, then she shoved it my way and moved behind the counter.

"Counterman's late. Coffee?"

"Please."

Claude Crawford was in custody until Betty Smallwood could raise two hundred fifty thousand dollars for bail. Even at ten dollars a pop, that would take a lot of notarizing. I didn't see it happening.

According to the paper, the physical evidence found at the scene of the murder linked both of the Crawfords to the crime, but Billy's lack of an alibi at the time of Nick's death made him the prime suspect. Billy had escaped by disappearing into the hills behind the abandoned factory on Route 123, where he'd been hiding. The media took that as an admission of guilt.

"You never know about people," the waitress said, bringing my coffee.

Apart from the occasional abduction they had committed, nothing I'd heard about the Crawfords suggested they were psychopaths. Why would they tell Lucy to talk to Nick and then kill him right before she did? Was it, as the waitress thought, just to get her as a reliable, non–Native American alibi? Or to get Nick's defenses down by having him think he was going to meet a good-looking woman instead of a man with a gun? And why do it at the hotel? There must have been a dozen less public places for the murder to happen.

Laurie sat down again and I offered her the paper back; she shook her head. "I'm finished. Too much sad news. You just never know. Billy always seemed like the nice one. We had a homeless guy freeze to death near the Dumpster two winters ago." She looked at me as if I should remember, so I nodded politely.

"Next week Billy shows up with a couple of cheap sleeping bags. Gave them to the old guys who scrounge around back there."

A woman hurried by the coffee shop. Laurie said hello but the woman didn't seem to hear and kept walking, her cowboy boots clacking on the tile floor as she rushed by.

"Now there goes one of the nice ones. Jackie Connelly. She and I went to high school together. A beautiful girl. Athlete. She could have gone to the Olympics. Got in a little trouble, but, you know, righted the ship. Kept her baby girl, finished school. She worked two, three jobs for years. Even cleaned houses so that child would never want for anything. Now she's got her own little one." It took me awhile before I realized the the baby that Laurie was talking about was Chantel Crawford.

Out of the corner of my eye, I saw two figures loitering by the elevator—one slim and one very large, in a leather jacket.

"Okay, that's it." The waitress didn't know what I meant.

I folded the paper and scribbled my room number on the check. Alone, on the highway, at night, it was one thing. But in a hotel lobby in broad daylight I felt safe enough to confront them. The big one had the nerve to smile at me. He had on sunglasses and a tweed bucket hat as a half-assed disguise but he wore an enormous black leather jacket like the one I remembered from our first encounter in the mini-mart.

"Can I help you two?" I said.

The men looked at each other stupidly as if they didn't know what I meant.

"You're not very good at keeping yourselves hidden. If you're going to sneak around following people you should try to be a little less obvious. The hat and the glasses? That's like we're not supposed to know Clark Kent is Superman because of his eyeglasses." More simpleminded looks.

"Forget it. The liquor store should be opening soon. Go get some more vodka, drink some courage, and then tell Sergei you saw me," I said, shaking my head in disgust. "But I want you to know I'm not scared of you. And if I ever see you again, I'll be armed," I said, thinking of the Taser and glad that I'd taken it from Babe.

By this time, my hands were shaking as I pushed the button for the elevator. Still, I felt good about standing up for myself and when the car came I swaggered inside and stood there glaring at them until the doors closed. Just as they did I heard one of the men say to the other, *"Bella ragazza, ma lei deve essere matta."*

Thirty-eight

"No, no, you don't understand. I've lost it. I verbally abused two Italians who are here to buy discount Fendi at the outlets."

Like a true friend, Lucy was sympathetic. "At least they thought you were beautiful." She stored the shopping info for later.

And *crazy,* if my Pimsleur Italian course served me well. I needed to get back to Springfield to my little garden business, where the only one chasing me was Caroline Sturgis, who'd left two more messages I hadn't had a chance to play.

Lucy called her producer to tell her the casino story had changed. Now that it was murder and not just racketeering they were even more interested. Her plan was to return with a cameraman in three days. In the meantime we'd visit Claude in jail and then get the hell out of Dodge.

"When did you wear the leather pants?" she asked as she watched me pack. In all the drama of Lucy's return, I'd forgotten about Oksana. I told Lucy about our meeting at the casino.

"You think she was in love with Vigoriti?" she asked.

"Crush, maybe. She's such a kid. And a little naive for someone who's seen as much as she has."

In the lobby I searched for Hector and Oksana. I didn't see them, but the ever-cheerful Amanda was there, measuring her corpse flower. I dragged Lucy over to say hello.

"So this is the famous corpse flower," she said, feigning interest. Amanda gave her the two-minute description of the titan arum. The girl was convinced the plant would bloom in the next twenty-four hours and be in flower for two days before it faded.

"Then it's really gonna smell like a dead body," Amanda said. "Not just like meat that's gone a little funky." She smiled as if she couldn't wait. "I've invited some of the kids from school for a Goth party in the bar when it does." I didn't know if selling a few extra beers to coeds with heavy eye makeup was Bernie's original plan when he agreed to host the corpse flower, but any extra business was not a bad thing.

Lucy had drifted; she wasn't really listening to Amanda and at that point neither was I.

"What's up?" I asked.

"I got it," Lucy said. "We shoot this for the piece on the murder. Listen, we were going to be here today anyway. Why don't we stay another night? I'll get a cameraman up here to shoot the party and I'll treat you to something from Fendi on the way home. Deal?"

If the sign of an enlightened mind is the ability to hold two contradictory beliefs at the same time, at that moment Lucy was enlightened. She hated herself for exploiting Nick's murder, but couldn't resist the attraction of a good story.

"We might be on television?" Amanda said. She grew red with

excitement. "Are you serious? Omigod, I have to call people. *Everyone* will come."

"Don't get too excited. It might not even make the final edit; I really want the plant." Lucy took out her business card and gave it to Amanda. "Can you give me some notice before this baby blooms?" Amanda was apoplectic with joy and nodded so furiously I thought she was going to do herself an injury.

At the front desk we told them we were extending for another day, and asked the bellman to bring our bags back to the room we'd just checked out of. Then we headed out for the county courthouse, where Claude was being held.

Driving back through Shaftsbury, we passed Georgie's convenience store. The Powerball jackpot was up to one hundred and eight million dollars; a few cars with New York and Massachusetts plates were parked outside, the owners loading up on tickets. The shades were down in Betty Smallwood's third-floor office.

In the absence of a metal detector, the desk sergeant at the courthouse simply asked if we had any guns, knives, pepper sprays, or sharp objects and he believed us when we said no. The prisoner was only allowed one visitor at a time, so I stayed outside in the waiting room while Lucy met with Claude.

I'd already seen the paper and the only other reading material was a two-year-old copy of *US* magazine; I was embarrassed that I knew the happy celebrity couple on the cover had, to use the magazine's terminology, already gone *splitsville.*

I walked around the small building reading the wanted notices: deadbeat dads and runaways mostly, a few foreclosure auctions, and the freshly minted poster of Billy Crawford, fugitive.

Behind me, someone else was subjected to the same gentle line of questioning as Lucy and I had been. *Who are you here to see? What are you bringing?*

"What about you, little guy? Are you smuggling anything in in that diaper?" The cop chuckled and playfully patted the baby's bottom. Then Chantel and Sean Crawford sat down on the bench next to me.

Thirty-nine

Chantel's face was clear, unlined, and unmade-up except for a thin blue stripe of eyeliner, which made her small eyes look even smaller. She wore skinny jeans tucked into fake Timberland boots and a fringed jacket that I'd seen for sale at my local Wal-Mart months ago while I'd been buying seeds. Her long curly perm was growing out and had reached the stage I remembered thinking of as "Tut head." That aside, she was pretty. And the kid was adorable—wide face, dark eyes, and straight dark hair, the kind of face you'd see in a baby food commercial.

I didn't know how many other prisoners there were in the county courthouse that day, but I thought I knew who she was there to see.

"Sweet little boy," I said.

"Thanks." After an awkward minute or two she asked me if I was there to see Claude.

"Yes and no. My friend is in with him. She's a journalist," I added, instantly feeling elitist for saying journalist and not reporter, even though strictly speaking Lucy was neither. "They're friends, sort of."

She nodded. "Claude's got a lot of women friends," she said, rolling her eyes. "He's my brother-in-law. Was, I guess. Is he still my brother-in-law if my husband is dead?"

Damned if I knew. Did it matter? She bounced the baby on her knee, alternately staring at the kid and then off into space. Even though I knew, I asked her name.

"Chantel."

"Pretty name."

"My mother was reading a romance novel when she was pregnant with me—one of the characters was named Chantel." She'd obviously told the story a hundred times before and delivered it with an equal measure of embarrassment and pride until she knew how the story would be received. I smiled.

"She doesn't even remember the name of the book. I guess I should be glad she wasn't reading *Harry Potter*. I coulda been called Frodo or something." So Mom was the reader in the family, not her.

"And who's this strapping fellow?" I asked, tugging on a tiny denim sleeve.

"This is my little Sean-ny."

His real name was Sean, after her favorite actor, Sean Penn. But Chantel thought Seanny sounded Indian, even though we were in the wrong part of the country for Shawnee. Chantel's husband, Bobby Crawford, had been killed in a house fire just before Seanny was born.

"They said he was drinking but I don't know. He promised he wouldn't . . . after we found out about Seanny. I think he just fell asleep with a cigarette, that's all. He was gonna try to stop that, too.

"Everything burned up in the fire. My mom let us move in for a while, got Seanny new baby things. She even got a lawyer to look into Bobby's insurance. I didn't care but she looked after us. She was thinking about Seanny. She said we had to make sure everyone knew Sean was Bobby's little boy. You know how some people talk when there's money involved."

"I think I may have seen your mother at Titans. Is her name Jackie?"

"That's her. She's real young. People sometimes take us for sisters." I was working on the math when Chantel told me her mother had only been sixteen years old when she gave birth.

"Mom was away from home, at a competition. My biological father was an athlete from another school. She never even told him. I mean what for? Was he supposed to drop out of high school and come marry some girl who lived two thousand miles away?"

It sounded like the mantra that Jackie Connelly must have repeated to herself and her little girl when they were both growing up.

"Anyway," Chantel said, "she had a good weekend. She just missed one double axel, otherwise she would have medaled."

Lucy finally came out and the sheriff's assistant ushered Chantel and baby Sean into the visitor's room.

"Was that . . . ?" Lucy asked, turning around to check Chantel out. "God, she looks so young."

"She is," I said. "How's Claude doing?"

Claude Crawford was doing well, considering he'd lost two brothers in six months. "He's got a warrior's attitude," Lucy said. If she was no longer in love, she was still infatuated. We walked out to the car and sat in silence for a few minutes. I gave her some time. She drove zombielike through the town until I made her pull over.

"I'm not getting on the highway with you like this, even for one exit," I said. "Let me drive and you tell me what happened in there."

There were no tissues in the rental car, just a stack of rough, coffee-stained Dunkin' Donuts napkins; they would have to do for the tears I knew were coming. She blotted her eyes to push the tears back, and then held up her bangs briefly, keeping the napkins there as if her head were about to explode.

"They wouldn't have even been at the hotel except for me. Neither would Nick. Nick might be alive if it wasn't for this stupid story. And who cares anyway if there's another casino in Connecticut? If people want to gamble they'll figure out a way to do it. Remember the Te-Adoros in Brooklyn?"

The waterworks started again and I flattened out more of the crumpled napkins for her to use.

I did remember the Te-Adoros. They were cheap cigars. Like Coca-Cola, the company gave large red and white signs to anyone who promised to carry their product. Seemingly overnight, dozens of independent stores with the same Te-Adoro signs opened up in Brooklyn and in addition to selling cigars, newspapers, and cigarettes, they did a nice business with illegal video poker machines discreetly tucked away behind the cases of soda and bottled water.

"It's all my fault," she sobbed.

"It's not." I didn't add that she, too, could have been killed by whatever lunatic had shot Nick, but presumably she knew that. At least in her more lucid moments. She took a deep breath. "Billy didn't kill Nick."

"And you know this because his brother told you? What possible motivation could he have for lying?"

"He's not lying. Billy and some homeless guy saw it happen.

Now that Billy's disappeared they'll say he did it. And the real killer will come after Claude because he thinks Claude knows."

"*Does* he know who the killer is?"

Lucy shook her head. Trying to keep his brother safe, Billy hadn't told him who he'd seen put a hole in Nick Vigoriti's head. I had my doubts as to whether Billy's strategy would work. Whoever killed Nick would want to make sure neither of the Crawford brothers talked, and you can't talk if you're dead. He'd also want to make sure Lucy didn't talk. And me. I opened the passenger-side door and walked around to the driver's side.

"Well, somebody knows. Slide over," I said. She looked at me through puffy, veiny eyes.

"Who?" she asked.

"Let's go find that homeless guy."

Forty

"We're going to Georgie's."

"It's starting to freak me out that you know everyone in this town after less than a week," Lucy said, checking herself out in the mirror and fixing her hair.

"I don't know everyone," I said. "It's a small town. People tell you their names and you remember them; it's not as if there are eight million of them."

I hadn't really expected the homeless guy to still be standing where I'd seen him yesterday, but Georgie's was as good a place to start looking as any.

"You mean Sam?" Georgie asked. Were there many homeless guys pushing Big Y shopping carts with American flags on them in this town? I said yes.

"That was a wonderful thing you did for him. I been telling everybody how you gave Sam a whole new start."

I don't usually give money to people on the street. In New

York, conventional wisdom says they'd only go straight to the liquor store with it and buy another bottle; here, it seemed different. But twenty bucks hardly qualified as a whole new start. "It was only a few dollars. Have you seen him?"

"Not since yesterday." He clammed up as if he thought I might be looking for change from the twenty.

"He might be in trouble," Lucy said.

"Scout's honor, I haven't seen him," Georgie said. "I kidded him, maybe he was going to Florida with all that dough."

And who would have blamed him if he did leave town. Especially if Sam suspected what *we* did: that Billy Crawford was being set up and hunted for what he'd seen that night, and thought he might be next.

I scribbled a note on the back of a business card and left it with Georgie. "If you see him, please ask him to call me. We're only trying to help.

"Is Betty Smallwood around?" I asked.

Georgie shook his head.

Betty had been running around trying to raise Claude's bail. He looked from me to Lucy and back again. "Were you the girl in here with Claude the other night?" he asked.

"That was me," Lucy said.

"Yeah, that Claude always had an eye for the ladies. You be careful now."

We left Georgie's and headed back to Titans, to see if anyone there had seen Sam/Big Y, the homeless guy who now had a real name.

Taylor, the clerk in the oversize jacket who was on duty the night I first arrived, was at the front desk. He was grinning and pleased with himself that he remembered my name.

"Hello, Ms. Cavanaugh. Welcome back to Titans."

Lucy answered him and the kid looked confused. Then she did. "Never mind," I told her, "it's too complicated."

I asked if he'd seen Hector and he told me Hector and Rachel had been in the bar when he came on duty.

"I don't know if they're still there. I only noticed because I like to keep an eye on Amanda when she's in the hotel." So he was the boyfriend.

I was in no hurry to see Rachel Page again and knew she wouldn't be helpful if we did see her. "Taylor, will you do us a favor?" He looked nervous, but Lucy picked up her cue and turned on the charm. "Will you call Mrs. Page's number and see if she's in her office? We don't want to disturb her if she's discussing important business with Hector." I felt sorry for deceiving the guy, but what harm would it do? He thought about it for a minute, then Lucy flashed her baby blues at him and he couldn't pick up the phone fast enough. Sometimes I hated her.

He put the phone on speaker and dialed. "Mrs. Page? Oh, there you are."

"You just called me, you halfwit. Who did you think would be here? What is it?" she asked. Taylor paused; he hadn't thought that far ahead and since the phone was on speaker we couldn't help him out. "Young man, are you trying to get fired?" She slammed the phone down.

Once we knew Hector wasn't with Rachel, we went into the lounge looking for him. He was at the far end of the bar, nursing what looked like an iced tea.

"You ladies just can't get enough of this place, can you? Or is it me?"

"Hey, Hector." We slid onto bar stools on either side of him.

"I like this. A Hector sandwich."

"Dream on. Do you remember the homeless guy who was

behind the hotel, near the Dumpster, the night Nick was killed?"

"Why?"

"C'mon. It's a simple question," I said, trying to sound tougher than I felt.

"Y. Big Y. We call him that because of the shopping cart."

Clever.

"I haven't seen him since that night. Some of Nick's friends were asking, too. They think he rolled the body before he reported finding it. Seems Nick had an expensive watch or something." Hector took a sip of his drink and I revised my first guess about what was in the glass. "Don't look at me like that, *mamí*, I'm off duty."

Having seen Sam recently—and not looking flush—I didn't buy it, but I said nothing to Hector.

"Is there anything else I can do for you ladies? Private tour of the grounds? The hot tub?" He knew the answer was no, so he finished his drink and left us sitting at the bar.

Lucy looked at me. "Now what?" she said.

I wasn't sure. I only knew two other places in town, the trailer park and the Crawfords' cabin on the mountain.

"You can forget about that cabin," Lucy said. "I've spent enough time there, thank you very much."

The bartender came over to see if we needed anything. I felt like a drink but didn't order one so we sat there with club sodas, as I had a few nights earlier when Nick Vigoriti was alive and Billy Crawford wasn't on the run. The bartender came back with a bowl of Goldfish.

"Did I hear you guys are looking for old Sam?" she whispered.

Forty-one

When you walk confidently and with purpose, people generally think you know where you're going and that you have every right to be there. So even though neither was true, that's how we strode through the first set of doors labeled Authorized Persons Only. Eventually we wound up in the same corridor that I'd been in with Hector and the cops when they brought me to identify Nick's body. Past two or three unmarked doors and a laundry room, where one of the busboys was folding tablecloths.

"Kitchen?" I asked.

"Around the corner."

By that time we could smell it. The kitchen was immaculate. Two men were busy chopping vegetables on gleaming stainless-steel surfaces when Lucy and I breezed through the Employees Only door, announcing to whoever might have cared that Helayne the bartender had said it was okay for us to enter.

My only experience with the kitchen at Titans had been a decent club sandwich, but the head chef and his staff looked like they knew what they were doing, at least to a woman whose idea of cooking was nuking a can of soup.

"Helayne doesn't run my kitchen. You two don't even have hairnets on. What the hell was she thinking?"

"We're not health inspectors and we don't want to get in your way, we just want to know if you've seen Sam," I said, talking fast before he had the time to kick us out.

At the mention of Sam's name, he softened, and walked us over to the sinks, where our long hair wouldn't get in any of the food. "Sam hasn't been here since the night of the murder and I'm worried sick. He was hunkered down, waiting by my van, the night Nick died. He looked terrible. I had two containers of food with me that I was taking to my mother. I gave them to Sam instead to tide him over until the police had cleared out. If I'd known he was going to be in the parking lot I would have brought more."

"Did Sam ever mention a hiding place, or someplace he went when it was too cold to stay outside?"

The chef shook his head. "He might have gone to Billy's cabin—if the police weren't looking for Billy." He was genuinely concerned. As the bartender had been.

"Sam must be a pretty nice guy for all of you to have tried so hard to help him."

"Years ago every kid in this town that wanted a summer job went to Sam," the chef said, smiling. "Sam would ask for a résumé and give them a formal interview and then always announce that they'd gotten the job. That's how we met. He was the foreman at a shoe factory, but it closed down eight or nine years ago."

That's when I knew what our next move was.

"You expect me to go to a deserted factory with you?" Lucy asked, out in the parking lot. She plucked a bite-size dinner muffin out of a doggie bag the chef had given her, and popped it into her mouth. "Are you nuts?"

"You went to a deserted cabin with a man you barely knew."

"That was different. Besides, I wouldn't have gone if I'd known there was a killer on the loose."

"I'm strapped." It was an expression I'd heard in a movie.

"I'm sorry, what did you just say?" Lucy said, wincing, and poking through the bag for more food.

"I have a weapon."

"I *know* what it means, I *took* you to that screening. When did you turn into Sarah freaking Connor?"

Inside the car, I showed Lucy the Taser, carefully sliding it out of the leopard-print case. I was getting more comfortable with it, especially since the cartridges were in my other pocket.

"Are you planning to shave the bad guy's legs?" Now that she mentioned it, it did look a bit like an electric razor.

"It's a Taser. Don't worry, Babe showed me how to use it this morning. Put your seat belt on."

"I feel so much better knowing you had a five-minute lesson on how to use a weapon with a former *backup singer*."

Still muttering, Lucy did as she was told and we went to find the factory. Now that we could charge her TomTom, we plugged it in and followed the disembodied voice as it instructed us to turn left and *take the highway, take the highway*.

"Why does this woman have to sound so snippy?" Lucy asked, playing with the TomTom and testing other voices. "Someone could make a bundle marketing one of these that sounded like George Clooney."

Our destination was less than seven miles away. TomTom/not

George chose the fastest route; it took us half a mile past the turn for the mobile park.

"If we don't find him, we can go back and ask some of the residents at the mobile park if they've seen him. He might have hitched a ride with one of them," I said.

"I want to find him, too, but you are officially on drugs. I am not going into a trailer park at this hour, ringing doorbells or whatever they have and asking if anyone's seen a homeless man with an American flag and a Big Y shopping cart. It's not happening."

"Then you and Claude have to hope we find him here," I said, pulling into the deserted parking lot.

The For Sale or Lease sign was faded from so many years in the sun, and the new banner's information that the owner was willing to subdivide the twenty-thousand-square-foot facility hadn't made it any more attractive to potential occupants. Except perhaps one.

Having seen the two-story property on the news, I recognized the spot where Billy Crawford had eluded the cops. "Let's circle the building first to see what looks promising," I said.

"Nothing looks promising. Let's go. This place is creeping me out."

We drove around to the back and parked, out of sight of the road. We tried all four doors to the building but they were locked.

"Satisfied? Now can we go?" Lucy said. The sun had gone down an hour ago and it had turned chilly; she rubbed her arms to warm them up.

"There," I said, pointing to an overturned trash can and the partially open window above it.

"There what?"

"That's where he goes in," I said.

Forty-two

The overturned drum made a lousy step and it was flaking and rusted in enough places to make me wonder when I'd had my last tetanus shot.

"Maybe Sam weighs less than we do," I said, half-joking.

"That's a depressing thought."

More likely he was just less fastidious about where he put his shoes, or maybe more confident that the crusted lime-green gunk on the drum wasn't toxic.

"The car. We'll move the car under the window and I'll stand on that to get in." I still had the rental car keys so I didn't wait for Lucy to agree. I kicked the drum over on its side, watching the dregs of the green gunk seep out through the bigger rust spots. Another kick moved the drum out of the way but not before punching a hole in it and spitting a gob of slime on my right pants leg.

Belgian blocks bordered a weedy strip underneath the window where I was sure that Sam had entered the building. The Subaru cleared the first block easily but its undercarriage scraped noisily over the second and third blocks.

"Good thing it's rented," Lucy said, practically.

I parallel-parked as close as I could to the side of the building, accidentally tapping the drum a couple of times before getting close enough.

"I'll go first," I said, as if there was any doubt. I climbed onto the hood of the car, then the roof. If I'd had the Jeep, getting in would have been a breeze, but the Subaru was lower to the ground and a longer way up to the windowsill.

I placed my bare hands on the splintered windowsill, wishing I had my heavy-duty work gloves. It took all of my strength to hoist myself up, lock my elbows, and shift my weight onto the windowsill. Thank goodness my Gravitron workouts had prepared me for this, although I rarely found broken glass in my local gym. I seesawed there for what seemed like minutes but was probably only seconds before I wriggled off the frame and dropped inside the building, tearing a nice hole in my hoodie in the process. Outside I could see Lucy pointing her phone at me and snapping pictures.

"You never know. Could be usable," she said.

"Are you coming?"

She made it to the top of the car, but after three tries still couldn't raise herself up to the windowsill or any place where I might have helped her get in.

"Okay, stay down there. If I'm not back in fifteen minutes dial Babe's number; I've got her phone. If I don't answer, get out of here and call the police." I walked away to look for Sam.

"Wait, what's her number?"

I gave it to her and she plugged it into their phone's memory.

"Wait," she yelled again, "you still have the car keys." I fished them out of my pocket and tossed them onto the roof of the car. They bounced off and landed in a puddle of ooze near the front tire.

"You know, this was supposed to be a free trip to a spa," I said. "So far, I'm not relaxed. You're going to have to get me something really nice at Fendi."

"Fifteen minutes," she said, looking at her watch. "And I *will* get you something nice."

Half of the windows were blacked out and the flood lights from the parking lot gave the floor the look of a checkerboard, light squares mixed with dark, for six feet or so until I reached the center of the floor, where it was pitch black.

"Sam? Sam? Can you hear me? My name's Paula. I was at the hotel the night Nick died." I heard a rustle and closed my eyes, briefly thinking, *Please don't let it be rats*. I heard it again and saw a line of giant water bugs conga-dancing across the floor.

"Your friends at Titans are worried about you. And Georgie, and Claude. Everybody's worried about you. I know you saw something. I was there that night, remember? Come on out, I can help you."

I ventured farther into the dark, waving my arms around, trying to avoid bumping into anything. Every once in a while I felt a cobweb on my face and that made me catch my breath. "Sam, are you here?" I was beginning to think he wasn't when I walked straight into the sharp edge of a piece of equipment, tearing a gash in my jeans and my thigh.

"Damn."

The next sound I heard built slowly, from a small creak to a thunderous explosion. A metal shelf unit filled with spare parts and lubricants for machines that no longer existed teetered, then came crashing down around me. The unit grazed my shoulder but there was no serious damage.

"Gee, Sam, was that on purpose?" I fiddled in my bag for the Taser, terrified that I would shock myself trying to load the cartridge.

"No. Just the vibration."

I followed the answer and saw him sitting in a corner on an old office chair. I couldn't place the smell, then it came back to me from my last camping trip. He reeked of Sterno.

"Let's get out of here before something else falls, okay?" I reached out a hand to him. He was surprised, but took it. I tried taking him to the window where I had climbed in but he resisted, and I wondered if I was going to have a problem getting him out of the building.

"Door's easier," he said, picking up a dirty red and white shopping bag and leading me to a door at the opposite end of the floor. Sam and I took the fire stairs two at a time until we reached a side door with a keypad lock that obviously hadn't been changed since the days when he worked at the factory.

Sam knew something was wrong before I did. Maybe you get used to a place—even an abandoned factory building—and can tell when something was out of whack as I'd been able to tell in my driveway, what was it . . . how many days ago?

One thing I did notice was different. Lucy's car was gone. And so was Lucy.

Forty-three

The cellular customer you are trying to reach is not available.

I'd try Lucy again later. She hadn't called but maybe the sound of the crash in the factory spooked her and she went for the cops. Sam and I waited for twenty minutes, then, by unspoken agreement, we started walking.

Ordinarily a seven-mile hike is a piece of cake for me; I'd made it to the top of Half Dome, for pete's sake, but I'd had a pretty full forty-eight hours and my thigh was bloody and throbbing from the cut. And my shoulder was aching from the shelf unit that had winged it. The road had virtually no shoulder and when the occasional car passed, it felt as if we'd be swept under the tires. There were no truckers, who probably would have stopped to help us, just a few kids who came too close, threw beer cans at us, and scared the crap out of me. But not Sam.

We'd walked about a mile when a car, already suspicious because it was going thirty-five with no one else on the road, pulled over fifteen yards ahead of us. The driver checked us out in his side mirror, then leaned out and asked if we wanted a ride.

It was amazing how much safer I felt with the C2 in my bag. I still hadn't fired the thing, but it gave me the confidence to say "Sure." Even so, I hopped into the backseat and let Sam ride up front. If I needed to whip out the Taser, being in the back would give me a little cover and it would be harder for the driver to see how scared I was to actually use it.

He had a plump face and that earmuff hairline—some back, some sides, no top. The suit was shiny and there were two suitcases with company stickers on them in the back. Salesman. He didn't seem to mind that Sam obviously looked like a homeless man and smelled like fuel, and I—face scratched, hoodie torn, green slime on one pants leg and blood on the other—didn't look or smell much better. And that suited us. All we wanted was a ride to Titans. A few minutes into the ride we found out why he didn't mind.

"Friends, I think you were put into my path for a purpose," he said with a smile. He waited for an acknowledgment.

Oh, brother. "And what would that be?" I asked, not really wanting to know.

"I'm here to snatch you from the road to perdition—literally and figuratively, heh, heh—and to set you back on the road to righteousness. You back there *can* stop your whoring and this man *can* stop his wretched drinking and fornicating and all you have to do is . . ."

What was he talking about? I couldn't speak for Sam but I hadn't whored and fornicated for a good year and a half. As a matter of fact, if I got through this experience alive, I planned to pick them up again with a vengeance. I tried tuning the driver out but he went on like that for six of the longest miles of my life. And each time his sermon reached a new crescendo he slowed down a bit for emphasis; we were going twenty-four excruciating miles an hour by the time we reached the turnoff for Titans.

"Stop the car. We can walk the rest of the way," I said. "It'll give us time to contemplate turning around our misspent lives."

At the speed we were going it wasn't dangerous so I opened the car door slightly and—worried that I'd jump out—the driver finally rolled to a stop. Clearly he hadn't finished his pitch and was annoyed by our early exit. I wondered if he had his spiel rehearsed and just cruised the highways at night looking for poor, unsuspecting hitchhikers to proselytize to.

As I got out he handed me some pamphlets from a religious group that I had never heard of but one that he assured me was chock-full of good American values. Sam gave the passenger-side door a stronger shove than I would have expected.

"Thank you, my friend," Sam said. "Can you spare a dollar to help me and the lady get a couple of coffees, to start our new lives of sobriety?"

"I won't do that," the driver said, with a smile. "You'll only spend it on drink." I didn't think Sam would, but I was ready for a strong one right about then.

"How about a reference? I'm a mechanical engineer and I think I recognize the corporate logo on your suitcases."

The driver hit the gas and took off, muttering some very unbrotherly words; Sam tossed the pamphlets after him and turned to me. "He obviously hasn't paid for his own drinks in a while if he thinks we're both going to catch a buzz for a dollar," he said. "T and E man. Probably cheats his company on travel and expenses."

The dirt road leading to the reservation and Titans just beyond it wasn't far. This time we talked.

"Sam, by all accounts you're a smart, likable guy. I gotta ask. What the hell happened?"

"Maybe I'll tell you the whole story one day. The short version is this . . . The company went under, all my savings were tied up in my 401(k). I borrowed money short-term at usurious rates to keep up my house payments, but I defaulted on the loans, and then lost my house. I lived in the trailer park for a while, but without a job even that got too expensive. It was surprisingly easy. And shockingly fast. I drank a bit after that." I could see why.

He was a walking news item. Something you hear about in a sound bite on CNN right before the story about the ferry accident in some part of the world you didn't know existed.

"No family?" I asked.

"No." There had to be a longer answer to that one but I didn't push it.

Near the entrance to the reservation two cars were parked nose to nose. At least three people were out of the cars and arguing. Sam grabbed my sleeve and raised a finger to his lips. He pulled me into the brush at the side of the road, and we crouched down to avoid being seen. The voices grew louder. A man's voice said, ". . . not what I signed on for . . ." and another said, ". . . you can go back to . . ."

I was staring straight ahead trying to make out any recognizable shapes or faces when a field mouse crept into my line of sight. We watched each other for about a minute, but I blinked first. The mouse ran around in circles, confused, and when he came close enough for me to see his little teeth I let out a yelp.

"What was *that*?" one of the threesome said.

Sam pulled two black lawn and leaf bags from his stash. "Put it over your head and curl up," he whispered. "Now!" He did the same.

A moment later the car in front of us moved and the one that was facing us turned its headlights on. We flattened ourselves farther into the brush.

"It's nothing, just the wind blowing some roadside garbage. Turn those lights off, you idiot." It was a woman's voice. And it was familiar.

Forty-four

In the last two hours I'd been bloodied, slimed, pelted with crushed beer cans, preached at, and mistaken for a bag of garbage.

"Do you go through this often?" I asked, once the cars had taken off and we climbed out of our bags.

"Almost every day. The lawn-and-leaf-bag trick saved my life once." Maybe twice, I thought, folding the bag and giving it back to him. I couldn't be entirely sure about whose voices I'd heard but they hadn't sounded happy and wouldn't have appreciated being interrupted.

"Any idea what kind of cars they were?"

"Too far to tell. But one was a smallish SUV, not a regular sedan."

That wasn't much help. Even Lucy's rental car was a smallish SUV. We walked the rest of the way to the hotel, passing the spot where the cars had been stopped. I looked around for a due.

"What are you looking for?" Sam asked. I didn't know myself;

It was as if I expected whoever it was to have left a calling card. But there were no convenient cigarette butts, candy wrappers, or vodka bottles, just some dusty tire tracks and a jumble of footprints.

"Just curious," I said. "You see anything?"

"Not much," Sam said. "I can tell you that one of them was a big man, size fourteen or fifteen shoes and probably pretty damn heavy." I couldn't believe what I'd heard. "I worked in a shoe factory, remember?"

Our plan was this: I'd enter the hotel through the main lobby, trying to keep a low profile until I got to my room. Sam would sneak in through the loading dock and take the freight elevator up to my room, where, hopefully, Lucy would be waiting for us. Then we'd try to reach Betty Smallwood for legal advice.

"You're not going to take off on me, are you? Look at me," I said, holding on to his arm. "I've gone through a lot to find you. Claude and Billy need you." He shook his head and I believed him.

We split up at the beginning of the long driveway into Titans. I kept close to the parked cars and in seconds, Sam had disappeared behind a hedge of green-and-white euonymus—clearly he'd done this before.

The valet parking attendant was asleep so I didn't have any trouble getting by him and through the revolving doors unnoticed. Unfortunately, Taylor, the friendly but perpetually confused desk clerk, was still on duty.

"Ms. Cavanaugh, gosh, are you all right?" I motioned for him to keep his voice down, but he was a teenage boy and that made my suggestion ludicrous. "Can I call a doctor for you?"

That got me more unwanted attention. One gentleman initially got up, ostensibly to offer his services, then demurred when he saw how bad I looked—visions of a malpractice suit, no doubt. I went to the front desk to shut up the well-meaning clerk.

"I'm fine." Now that he'd blown my hopes of sneaking into the hotel unnoticed, I decided to ask him for a favor. "Taylor, do you have a locker here?" He nodded. "What's in it?"

"A T-shirt, a sweatshirt, jeans, and sneakers. Old stuff, nothing nice," he said, still confused.

"Good." I looked through my handbag and pulled out my wallet. "I'll give you a hundred dollars if you send someone to my room with your clothes in five minutes."

"I could call Amanda. She's coming back later, so she could bring you something to wear."

"I need men's clothing."

"Oh, sure, I get it," he said knowingly. "We have a few other customers who like to do that, too. There's one guy, you should see him, wig and everything."

"A hundred dollars and you'll eventually get them back," I said, handing him the cash.

Forty-five

The elevator doors had just opened when I heard Lucy's scream. Sam flew past me and I grabbed him and hustled him back to the room before any other guests came out into the corridor to see what the disturbance was. After a few deep breaths, Lucy calmed down and apologized.

"It wasn't you. It was me," she said. "I was expecting Paula."

"No offense taken," Sam said, sitting down on the love seat and putting his shopping bag on the floor.

"That's a Michael's bag."

"It is. Good company. I used to own stock."

Lucy did her best to hide her surprise at both Sam's articulate answer and his obvious ease with the situation.

"What happened to you?" she said to me. "You look like shit."

"Thank you, I've been hiding in a Hefty bag. Why did you leave? We had to hitchhike back. You should have heard the psycho that picked us up."

What she did hear was the crash of the metal shelving unit inside the factory. She immediately called the cops and they told her to get the hell out of there and wait for them at Titans.

"That's what I did, about an hour ago, but they haven't come yet. They're probably at the factory looking for you two," she said.

"They didn't show up when we were there," I said. "Who did you call?"

"I called 911. Who do you get when you call 911?"

"A dispatcher," Sam said. "Up here they get a lot of prank calls so they make you jump through hoops to make sure it's really an emergency."

"Oh, I think from the way I was shrieking a perceptive person would have been able to tell that this was the real thing."

Sam smiled. "Any chance there's a Diet Coke in that mini-bar?"

"Mother's milk," Lucy said, and got up to get them each a can. "You two get acquainted. I desperately need a shower and a change of clothes. Sam's new clothing should be up in a few minutes. But don't scream when it is delivered. We don't want to attract any more attention."

I stripped a pillowcase from the bed and retrieved the leather pants and sleeveless top from my overnight bag and took them into the bathroom. The hoodie and top pulled off easily but the pants were glued to my leg with my own dried blood. Yanking them off hurt like hell, but I did it quickly the way you'd pull off a Band-Aid. The blood started flowing again and I stepped into the tub to catch it.

The shower felt great until I made a tactical error and let my thigh get hit by a direct stream of water. I let out a scream that rivaled Lucy's. I shifted positions and resigned myself to the fact that my right side would be cleaner than my left.

The gash was ragged but not that deep—my jeans had saved me a few layers of skin. Using the cuticle nippers in my travel kit, I started a hole in the pillowcase, then tore it into strips to make a bandage. I did a pretty good job; I looked like a professional tennis player with her thigh wrapped before a big match. I held my hairbrush like a tennis racket, spinning it around in my hands the way the pros do. I even took a few practice swings before realizing how idiotic it was for me to have left my best friend in the next room with a homeless man while I stood, naked, in the bathroom, practicing my serve.

I slipped into my pants carefully, grateful that the tight leather would hold the bandage in place. Sam and Lucy seemed to be having a lively conversation outside so I took an extra few minutes to put on makeup, rubbing tint on the apples of my cheeks. No need to look totally hideous.

When I emerged, towel-drying my hair, they'd been joined by a third person.

"You specifically told me not to scream," Lucy said through gritted teeth.

"Sit down."

And I did, since I make it a point never to argue with a woman who's got a gun.

Forty-six

"Good to see you," I said. "Thanks for returning my jacket." Lucy and Sam were less sure that it was good to see Oksana since she was clearly upset and holding a gun.

"Everything's gone wrong," she said, eyes weepy, waving the gun around the room. She repositioned the heavy leather messenger bag strapped across her chest and, in doing so, managed to point the gun at everyone in the room. "I'm not even supposed to be here."

"Feel free to leave," Lucy said. I shot her a look that suggested it wasn't smart to be a wiseass to a fairly hysterical person with a weapon.

Oksana had been fired. When the *friend* learned Oksana couldn't pay her share of the rent she'd been locked her out of the mobile home. With no other place to go she returned to Sergei, who'd asked for payment of a different kind.

Sam was sympathetic. "I know how it is," he said, "when it

seems like everything's gone wrong. But you're so young. You'll wake up tomorrow and see the world hasn't come to an end. And you'll go on. Believe me. Sit down and try to relax."

"Forgive me, but who are you?" she asked, doing as Sam had suggested.

"Sam Dillon." I wondered when he'd last used his entire name. Of course, the name meant nothing to her. "People at the hotel sometimes call me Big Y," he said. At that her eyes widened even further.

"You're Big Y? Is Billy here, too?" She stood up and looked around nervously. "You've got to get out of here. *All* of you. Sergei and his men are looking for you. He was hired to make sure nothing interfered with the casino deal. Nick tried to butt in and look at what happened to him."

After years of being a gofer for the Mishkins, Nick wanted to cash in. When he couldn't he threatened to go to the press with a story that would have had the hotel's investor on the first boat back to China and maybe even queer the Quepochas' chances for recognition.

"Sergei saw Nick talking to me and thought I was a reporter, right?" I said. Oksana nodded. "Did he have someone follow me to Springfield and search my house?"

"Could be Vitaly. And Marat. I heard Sergei tell them to check your computer. But not at the hotel because then the cops might suspect something." She rubbed her runny nose on the back of her hand, the one that held the gun.

"Wouldn't you like to put that gun down?" I said.

She acted as if she hadn't heard me. Sam nonchalantly reached for his can of soda and moved a little closer to Oksana, ready to make a move if necessary.

"They were supposed to reason with Nick, not kill him. I

don't know what happened. And then, then . . ."—she closed her eyes briefly—"Sergei asked me to find out how much you knew. I didn't want to be involved. I liked Nick, but I owe Sergei my life."

"What did you tell him?"

"That you knew nothing about the Mishkins' loan, the casino, or any of this business, that you were nice." She wanted me to believe her and I wanted to, but she was a practiced liar, and whether she'd admit it or not, Sergei clearly had a Rasputin-like hold on her. "I told him it was another woman . . . named Lucy." She looked at Lucy and raised her shoulders as if to apologize.

"Now he thinks I lied to him and they are after me, too. These people would just as soon kill you for fifteen hundred dollars as they would for fifteen million." Fifteen million dollars was indeed a powerful motivator. If Sergei thought he could get his hands on that kind of money, who knew what he'd be capable of? Oksana had sensibly taken the gun from Sergei's building for protection.

"Well, if it makes any difference, you didn't lie to him," Lucy said. "That's exactly why I was meeting Nick. After I saw the Crawfords." The realization dawned on Lucy's face; her fling with Claude may have saved her life. Talk about friends with benefits.

I tried to think of a way out of the hotel that would help us avoid Sergei and his men, if they were, in fact, looking for us. "Oksana, how did you know we were back at the hotel?"

"When that bitch Rachel Page fired me I asked Helayne to put my personal things in a bag. I was picking it up and she said she saw you." Yeah, it was hard to stay under people's radar when you were covered with blood and slime.

I was racking my brain to come up with a plan when our exit strategy knocked on the door. Lucy leaped out of her seat. Sam covered Oksana's gun with his hand. "Let's keep this out of sight, okay?" She agreed and put the gun in her hobo bag, which looked as if it was stuffed with all of her belongings.

A young girl in heavy Goth makeup was at the door. She held a bundle of clothing, my hundred-dollar rental from Taylor, the desk clerk. She looked around the room and saw a homeless guy dressed in rags; a model-thin Ukrainian girl with tear-streaked makeup; Lucy, nervously hopping from one foot to another; and me, barefoot in tight leather pants.

"So, are you guys dressing for the party?" she asked cautiously.

"Say it again?" I said, recognizing the voice but not the look.

"It's me, Amanda." The corpse flower had bloomed, and so, apparently, had she. The blond, blue-eyed homecoming queen who'd been recording the growth of the corpse flower was wearing white foundation, thick black eye makeup, leather wrist cuffs, and a cadaverous expression. The bicycle chain formerly used to lock the greenhouse was now doubled around her waist and tied off prettily with the lock.

"I called you," she said to Lucy, "but the line was busy. The whole school is downstairs. We're going to be partying all night in the lobby. Is this your cameraman?" Amanda asked, looking at Sam.

"One of them," I lied.

"These are pretty good outfits, but it's not really Goth unless you make your faces a little whiter. I have white shoe polish if you like."

So much for the rosy glow artfully applied to the apples of my cheeks; I asked her in.

Forty-seven

Sam showered and changed into Taylor's borrowed clothing while Oksana, Lucy, and I transformed ourselves into a trio of zombie extras from *Night of the Living Dead*. When the shoe polish ran out we relied on Lucy's gray eye shadow to sculpt the requisite lines on our faces.

"Do you have any idea how much this stuff costs?" Lucy asked.

"Do you have any idea how much funerals cost?"

"Good point," she said, slathering the precious Chanel cream in the hollows of her cheeks instead of on her eyelids. She bravely put on my skanky torn hoodie and gave it a few more rents for good measure; I borrowed Amanda's bicycle chain and wrapped it around my own waist, tucking the lock and key in my pocket as if they were a grant watch fob.

Sam had borrowed a disposable razor and elastic hair band from me and when he emerged from the bathroom he looked like a reasonably attractive, if emaciated, ponytailed fifty-year-old in jeans and T-shirt. I didn't want to think about how long it had been since he'd had a shower, and I was glad housekeeping would be cleaning the tub and not me.

"You women look damn scary. Have I really been out of circulation that long?"

"It's a party," Amanda said. "Not real life." She looked him up and down. "The other outfit was edgier. You look too healthy, now." Probably not something that Sam Dillon had heard in a while. He put on Taylor's UConn sweatshirt and we each contributed a little white stuff from our arms to smear on Sam's face. Not that anyone would have recognized him.

On the way to the party, we checked one another out. If we'd had more time Amanda said she would have painted our nails black, but as it was, we convinced ourselves we could pass for college students if the lobby was crowded, the lights were down, and no one looked too closely.

We needn't have worried. I couldn't imagine that even at the height of its popularity, Titans was any more crowded than it was when the elevator doors opened. It seemed as if the entire student body of the local UConn campus was in the hotel lobby dressed in black and drinking beer around the now-blossoming corpse flower.

Only Titans's employees were not in whiteface and Goth accoutrements and they stuck out like basketball players at a Pygmy convention. That's why it was easy to spot the Michelin Man. He'd positioned himself in the lounge and was so clearly not celebrating that the partygoers, not sensing a kindred spirit, gave him a wide berth.

"Let's not rush to the door," I said. "I don't want to be too obvious."

The corpse flower was spectacular and Amanda, or someone, had opened both doors and all of the panels to the greenhouse so that the cadaverous scent filled the lobby. She disappeared into the crowd to play hostess.

Before I realized it, I'd been separated from Lucy and Sam by a swarm of Marilyn Manson and Kelly Osbourne look-alikes in chain-mail tank tops. I didn't risk calling out their names and alerting the Michelin Man.

Someone took my arm. "Come with me." Marat, the Michelin Man's skinny sidekick, squeezed my elbow and pressed something hard and cold into my rib cage. The squiggly lines in his eyes had brothers on his cheeks and nose and he smelled like an ashtray. Only a drunk or an idiot would think that blowing me away at a hotel party was a smart thing to do but I wasn't going to bet my life on either this guy's sobriety or his brains. I went with him.

"Where are we going?" I asked.

"Shut up and walk. My boss wants to see you."

Who was his boss? The Michelin Man? Sergei? He led me through the lobby, past the freight elevator, and into the bowels of the hotel, where I'd been before, once with Hector and more recently when I'd visited the kitchen. I dragged my feet trying to remember which of the doors marked Employees Only led to the loading dock and which led to the kitchen.

"Can't you walk any faster?"

"It's the shoes," I lied.

"American woman are like sheep. They wear stupid clothing and stupid shoes. If you were in my country you'd be wearing good sturdy boots."

I was willing to bet that he hadn't seen Mother Russia for quite some time, if ever, and styles had changed, but I wasn't going to play What Not to Wear with him. Then I recognized the laundry room with its locked door. I smelled food and knew the kitchen was close by around the corner on the left.

When we made the turn I pushed my way into the kitchen with the skinny guy hanging on.

"Hey, this is my kitchen! Oh, it's you. Did you find Sam? Is he all right?" The chef looked from me to my attacker and quickly realized this wasn't a social call. The slightest tilt of his chin led my eyes to the kitchen knives on an island six feet to his right. Mine and the Ukrainian hood's.

"Can you throw a knife as fast as I can shoot?" Marat asked. "I don't think so." He was cackling at his own joke when one of the busboys came up from behind and hit him in the head with something shaped like a paddle. He fell to his knees and I was able to kick the gun out of his hand. It slid across the floor and wound up underneath one of the massive commercial ovens.

"Should I hit him again?" the busboy asked. He was standing over the now horizontal man ready to whack him again with a frozen Alaskan Salmon.

"No!" I didn't want him dead, just neutralized. "Do either of you have the key to that laundry room outside?" The chef nodded and produced a large key ring.

We draped a tablecloth over the man, just in case anyone was in the corridor, dragged him out of the kitchen, and locked him in the laundry room.

"Mrs. Page has the only other key," the chef said. "He'll stay in there until you tell me to let him out."

I ran back through the empty corridors to the hotel lobby. The party was in full swing now. I scanned the crowd for Lucy and Sam and saw them being ushered out by the Michelin Man, one upper arm in each of his hammy hands.

Someone in the crowd squealed and the Michelin Man spun around to look. I grabbed the nearest guy and planted a wet one on him to hide my face until I was sure the coast was clear.

"Whoa, thanks, lady. Do I know you?" *Lady*? Great. Here I was convincing myself that I could pass for a college student, and even wearing Goth makeup I was *lady*.

"Dude, I'm being cougared!"

I fished around in my bag and got out Babe's Taser. I loaded the cartridge just the way she'd shown me.

"Don't get me wrong. Cougar's not an insult, it's just, like, you know, an older fox." That was an ego boost. "You can kiss me again."

"Maybe later, sonny." I checked the safety twice then put the Taser in my pocket and ran out to the parking lot. The three of them were getting into the Toyota.

"Stop," I yelled, running toward them. I tried to keep the bicycle chain from flapping against my wounded thigh but was only intermittently successful. I considered tearing it off, but it was my backup weapon in case the Taser failed.

"Excellent," the Michelin Man said, "now we're all here." He tightened his grip on Lucy. "Just come quietly, we're all gonna have a nice little talk."

I crept closer to him and tried to stay calm. I knew I had to be fifteen feet away or less for the Taser to work. Once I was within range I spoke. "I'm not going anywhere with you, a-hole. And neither are my friends."

With one hand still pinning Sam to his side he shoved Lucy in the car and reached for something in his right pocket. Lucy kicked at his crotch and missed but it distracted him just long enough so that I could draw quicker.

"Move your leg!" I yelled. Then I fired.

Lucy screamed as the large man fell backward and rolled over. She scrambled out of the car, still kicking, and tripped over his inert body.

"Quick," I said, running toward her. "I don't know how long this thing lasts." I unwrapped the bicycle chain from my waist and used it to tie the Michelin Man's hands together. The three of us dragged him to the front of the car and locked the chain around the bumper.

Then we called the cops.

Forty-eight

Sam and Lucy huddled together; she was still shaking. I stood off to the side leaning on a parked car, staring at the Michelin Man, willing him back to life after the shock from the Taser. *C'mon, get up.* I reminded myself that I'd had to do it. Slowly, he came around. He reflexively jerked his hands up and yanked at the bumper, but he was at a bad angle and all he succeeded in doing was whacking himself in the chin. Just then two cruisers arrived, followed by Stacy Winters, who climbed out of an unmarked car.

"Relax, Vitaly." Winters gave the bottom of his foot a sharp kick. "You're only embarrassing yourself." He gave up and seemed to deflate visibly like a balloon with a slow leak.

She walked past him, shook a few Tic Tacs into her hand, then offered some to me.

"No thanks. Bad for the teeth."

"Are you sure the only things you dig up on a regular basis are plants? Because I do believe you caught yourself one of the perpetrators," she said, popping the mints into her mouth.

There was a tinge of grudging admiration in the remark and I couldn't resist bragging. "There's another one locked in the laundry room in the hotel."

"And the head cheese?" she asked.

"Still at large."

"Not for long. My men just went around the back of the hotel to seal off that exit. Bernie won't get away." She chewed on the Tic Tacs and shook out some more.

"Bernie Mishkin?"

Winters ticked off her reasons. "He had the means, the opportunity, and fifteen million motives."

Bernie's Chinese investor knew all about the hotel's precarious financial situation, but his people hadn't been able to navigate the byzantine workings of Congress and the Bureau of Indian Affairs. Bernie had convinced them the Quepochas' federal recognition was imminent. And with that would come casino gambling and busloads of tourists from New York and Boston eager to leave their money in the Nutmeg State.

"How could he promise them that? He's not a Native American," I said. "Is he?" I remembered what Betty had said about membership in the tribe.

"He's not, but Daniel Smallwood is." Winters thought the two of them had cooked up a scheme to defraud the investors. Fifteen million dollars would go a long way toward paying off the Mishkins' bills *and* keeping the tribe's case in court for years to come. It wouldn't matter if the Quepochas were never recognized.

"Why wouldn't Daniel Smallwood just do this on his own? Why did he need Bernie?" I asked.

"They gave each other credibility. And they convinced this Wai Hi that they could earn the cost of a new hotel's construction with one year's worth of gaming revenues from Bernie's old hotel."

"You think Nick was going to blow the whistle and one of them killed him?"

"I think they hired someone to do it." She pointed to the Michelin Man, who was still shaking off the effects of the Taser and scratching the spot where the barbs had hit him.

"I didn't kill nobody," he said. "That's not what I signed on for. I want my lawyer."

"Maybe him, maybe Billy Crawford, we're not there yet. But we will be soon."

I asked her about the evidence they'd found that implicated the Crawfords. She hesitated for just a second. I could almost see her thinking, *Why the hell not?*

"Hair," she said.

Sam looked up. That was all she said before walking away toward the hotel.

The cops asked me for the key to the bicycle lock. They unchained the Michelin Man, cuffed him, and read him his rights, squashing him into the cruiser, where he took up most of the backseat.

"This is police brutality. I should be in a van. I want my lawyer."

"Shut up, Vitaly," one of the cops said, bored. He returned the chain and lock to me and I draped it around my neck, putting the key in the lock for safekeeping.

For thirty minutes the cops interrogated us.

"We struggled. I kicked him," Lucy said, skirting around the issue of the Taser; a good thing since none of us knew what Connecticut laws were regarding Tasers.

Remarkably, they believed the three of us managed to subdue

a three-hundred-pound thug. They'd know the truth soon enough but I didn't feel the need to volunteer that information, not just yet. If the Michelin Man was smart enough to ask for his lawyer, maybe I'd wait for mine.

While we were outside answering questions, we could hear Amanda's goth party still going strong. The corpse flower was a huge success; somewhere Fran Mishkin must have been smiling. I doubted whether any of the students even noticed a scrawny, twitchy guy being freed from the hotel's laundry room and brought out in cuffs to join his fleshy friend on the way to jail in the back of a second police cruiser. Minutes later, Bernie and Rachel were led out of their hotel, Bernie, in cuffs covered by a jacket, blubbering on about the newspapers, and Rachel, two steps behind, as usual.

Hector Ruiz stood in the doorway and assured them he had the situation under control and all publicity was good publicity. I wasn't sure that adage extended as far as an accusation of murder, but what did I know—Hector was a pretty sharp cookie.

Sam, Lucy, and I watched them all drive off until we were alone in the parking lot.

"I don't know about anyone else, but I could use a drink," Lucy said. She marched ahead of us into the crowded lobby.

Sam passed. He'd been sober for four hours and said he was shooting for five. Then six. One hour at a time, then one day at a time. He wouldn't take any money. "I bought a few Powerball tickets with that twenty you left for me. I never got a chance to thank you."

"It's been a pleasure meeting you, Sam. Take care of yourself." I didn't know what else to say. "If you ever want any part-time landscaping work, give me a call, okay?" I wished him luck and leaned in for the double back pat—friendlier than a handshake but not as intimate as a kiss.

"You look good, baby," Sam whispered.

I said a quick prayer that the night wouldn't get any weirder than it had already been. Granted, Sam had cleaned up pretty good and I didn't like to think of myself as a snob, but was this an appropriate time for a pass? I froze and said nothing. I hoped I wasn't wincing at what I thought was an untimely suggestion.

"Billy brought me a jacket that night. We met on the loading dock." That might be why Billy's hair was found at the scene. "We heard someone coming. Billy wasn't supposed to be there, so we hid behind the Dumpster. I couldn't really see; Billy was closer. But I heard them. *You look good, baby.* That's what Nick said to the woman right before she shot him." Then Sam disappeared again behind the hedges.

I walked through the party, into the bar, stunned. If Sam was right and the killer was a woman, there was a short list of suspects. And the one at the top of the list used to work for Sergei and was last seen wearing my black quilted jacket.

"What's the matter?" Lucy said. "You look pale. Oh, wait, we all look pale." There were already two rings on the bar in front of her and she called the bartender over to order a drink for me.

I didn't recognize the girl behind the bar but she stared as if she knew us. "Is one of you Paula?" she asked, with a faint accent. I toyed with the idea of saying no; after all, one of us wasn't.

"That would be me," I said, exhausted, holding up my hand.

"I have something for you." My whole body tensed. I hoped it wasn't a shot to the face. Being half-Italian, my family was big on open caskets.

She pulled a plastic drugstore shopping bag out from under the bar. "Oksana left this for you." It was my quilted jacket.

I let out a nervous laugh. "Hey, old friend, I never thought I'd see you again." I put the jacket on, turned up the collar, and dug my hands in the pockets, modeling it, QVC style. In one of the pockets I found a note. I unfolded the slip of paper and read it out loud.

Dear Paula,

If you are reading this I hope it means that you and your friend are okay. Billy and I are going away to someplace where Sergei cannot find us. Where we can start fresh. It wasn't Sergei's fault. It was that woman. He never would have needed so much money if she hadn't talked him into buying that damn Zamboni. Wish us luck.

Oksana

Lucy nearly coughed up an olive. "Holy shit. Well, she finally found someone to look after her. But what the hell is a Zamboni? It sounds like an Italian pastry—*leave the gun, take the Zamboni.*"

"It's a very expensive machine used to clean and smooth the ice at a skating rink," I said, putting two and two together.

"Are there many skaters around here?" she asked.

I knew of two, Viktor Petrenko, the former Olympic gold medalist, and Jackie Connelly, who blew a double axel at a high school competition twenty-four years ago and was comforted by an athlete from a school two thousand miles away. Something told me Petrenko wasn't involved.

Forty-nine

It made sense. Sergei and Jackie were both looking to hit the jackpot, and they had something in common: ice.

"The waitress at the coffee shop told me that as a single mom Jackie frequently held two or three jobs just to keep a roof over their heads. She even worked as a maid. Shaftsbury's a small town in a small county—how many cleaning services can there be around here? Jackie probably met Sergei at work. The skating rink must have seemed like a way to get back to the life she thought she'd have when she was a kid." I downed my drink.

"Until the cannoli broke down," Lucy said, she was more than a little tipsy.

"*Zamboni.* No more drinks for you. When that didn't work out Jackie jettisoned Sergei and aimed higher," I said. "What if Jackie tried to involve her son-in-law in some scheme and he said no?"

"The guy who died in the fire?"

I nodded. "Bobby Crawford. He and Nick were friends. Maybe Nick found out about the scam and that's what he was going to tell you the night he got killed. Maybe Bobby's death wasn't an accident."

"So what do we do now?"

"We call the cops, like normal people. But only when we get the hell out of this hotel," I said. "I don't know who to trust anymore except for you." I looked around as suspiciously as Oksana had that night in the casino.

Back on the Merritt, we stopped for diet Red Bulls. They didn't really go with martinis, but Lucy had had three drinks and I'd had one, and I wanted to stay awake and not drive us into a ditch. At the service station's minimart, I'd call Winters and tell her what we'd learned.

Lucy entered the market and I was just about to dial Stacy's number when I saw what looked like my own Jeep, blue tarp flapping in the wind, speeding in the opposite direction. I tried to flag it down. It didn't take me long to figure out what was happening. So I ran into the market to tell Lucy.

"I never called Babe; I think I saw her driving back to Titans."

The clerk's eyes were wide and his mouth hung open. Two agitated women in Goth makeup were loading up on highly caffeinated drinks and appeared to be on the lam. Were we dangerous? Were we the ghosts of Thelma and Louise ready to knock over his Plexiglas cubicle? I tried to reassure him.

"It's okay, Ravi. We just need a couple of drinks," I said.

"How do you know my name?" he shrieked. "Take whatever you want!"

"Chill. Your name's on your shirt." I peeled off a few dollars, then hurried Lucy out of the store, but not before sticking my head back in and telling the frightened clerk to have a nice day.

"What did Stacy say?" Lucy asked, straightening up and popping open a can.

Damn. I still hadn't called. I tried her number but it was busy. Then I speed-dialed Babe's other number from the phone she'd given me.

"Where the hell are you?" she said.

"On the Merritt. Did you just pass the Mobil station?"

She had. I told her to turn around and meet us back there.

"All right, but it may take a while, the next exit isn't for miles."

We still hadn't called Winters so I told her we'd wait. And we would have if a blue Isuzu hadn't pulled into the service station's lot inches away from Lucy's rental car, effectively blocking the driver's-side door.

Jackie Connelly wasn't as afraid to use the gun as I'd been to use the Taser. Of course, she'd had more practice. She forced us into the wooded area past the place where families on long car trips stopped to picnic or walk their dogs. But not at this hour of the night.

"I wouldn't let Nick screw this up," she said, "and I'm certainly not going to let you two. Keep walking."

Between the martinis and the uneven surface, Lucy stumbled and I held on to her to keep her on her feet. Every once in a while, Jackie prodded me in the back to make me speed up. I tried blaming the shoes again, but she was smarter than Marat and made me kick them off.

"I've been waiting a long time for a break like this. I wasted five years with Sergei. Helping him start those two-bit companies. I wasn't going to waste another five waiting for him to fix his Zamboni."

Jackie thought she'd gotten her break when Chantel married Bobby Crawford. She went to him with a plan to wring money out of the casino backers. They'd be playing to the investors' greed. People like that deserved what they got, she'd said. And chances are the casinos would never even be built. But Bobby didn't go for it. Neither did Bernie Mishkin.

"All my life I've been surrounded by underachieving men," Jackie said. "That's why I finally went to Rachel."

I knew the more she told us, the more she'd feel she had to kill us, but she just kept talking. I fingered the phone in my pocket, wondering if I could hit redial or 911 so at least someone could hear our last words, but the phone was Babe's and had an unfamiliar keypad.

"What are you doing?" she asked, poking me in the back again.

"It's my rosary."

"Bullshit. It's a phone. Hand it over."

"My phone's in my handbag. You can have it." I took my time and walked toward her barefoot, sidestepping the petrified dog poop. I fumbled in my bag for the Taser, found it, and slid back the safety cover.

"That's close enough. Don't forget I've got your drunken friend here." She pointed the gun directly at Lucy.

In the dark, the way I held it, the leopard-print Taser even looked like a phone. I pretended to hand it to her but pressed it to her arm instead. She dropped in an instant.

I grabbed Lucy and we ran back to the car. Then we heard the sirens. In the Jeep, Babe jumped the curb and screeched to a halt right near us, having seen some of the action in the headlights. A state trooper's car followed because Babe had hopped a divider to get to us faster. And Ravi hadn't been fooled by my *have a nice day*; he'd called the cops like any normal person would.

Jackie Connelly was in the back of the trooper's car and the weapon she'd pulled on Lucy and me had been retrieved by the time Stacy Winters arrived. Rachel Page had broken down and confessed to fraud but vehemently denied any involvement in Nick's murder.

"She couldn't watch baby brother go to jail for something she'd done. She gave us plenty on Jackie though. And Sergei. Although the elusive Mr. Russianoff seems to have disappeared. No one's seen him for the last four days."

"And the Smallwoods and the Crawfords?" I asked.

"In the clear," she said. "Jackie orchestrated this beautifully. Manipulating Sergei, getting him and Rachel to do her dirty work, and throwing suspicion on anyone who got in her way."

"As long as you've got her in custody, you might want to ask her about the fire at Bobby Crawford's," I said.

Stacy was impressed. "All right, maybe you're not the pain in the ass I thought you were."

Once I found my shoes, I'd take the Jeep and Babe would drive Lucy's rental car back to Springfield. I poked around in the dog run.

"Come here," Babe said, calling me over to the side of the car, "I've got something to tell you."

"Only if it's good news or funny," I said. "I've about had all the excitement I can handle for one night."

"You know Caroline Sturgis has been trying to reach you. She's got an idea she wants to talk to you about."

"I've got an idea too," I said. "I know a great diner about twenty minutes from here, and I'm pretty sure it's still open."

Epilogue

The gun found on **Jackie Connelly** was identified as the same gun used to kill **Nick Vigoriti**. She is awaiting trial for his murder.

Rachel Page confessed to falsifying documents related to the sale of the Titans Hotel to the Quepochas tribe for the purposes of defrauding foreign investors. The state is currently determining what charges will be brought against her.

Bernie Mishkin was cleared of all charges, but his Chinese investor was scared off and pulled his money off the table. In Fran's honor he kept the corpse flower.

Amanda Bornhurst was hired part-time as an event planner for the hotel, and has since run three successful parties, contributing to Titans's first profitable quarter since 1986.

Hector Ruiz was promoted to director of publicity and marketing, chiefly on the strength of his assertion that he could get Jennifer Lopez and Marc Anthony to agree to appear at the hotel. They have yet to perform but the attendant publicity has raised the profile of the hotel and increased business by 12 percent.

Sam Dillon used some of the twenty dollars I gave him to buy a handful of lottery tickets. He won one of the state's single biggest Powerball payouts and is planning to reopen the shoe factory and rehire some of the old workers. He's been sober for fourteen months.

I got a postcard from **Oksana Smolova** and **Billy Crawford** from the Four Corners area. They have opened a motel and have no plans to come back to Connecticut.

Sergei Russianoff's decomposing body was found six months later in an abandoned skating rink in Simsbury, Connecticut. Jackie Connelly claims she knows nothing about it but she is considered a prime suspect.

Lucy Cavanaugh and **Claude Crawford** are working on a screenplay covering the events at the Titans Hotel. They have interest from a VP at Paramount providing **Chantel Crawford** agrees to let baby **Sean** appear in the film. She's agreed. **Betty Smallwood** brokered the deal.

The *Springfield Bulletin* ran the feature on the Hawley family quilt. I never volunteered to write another article for the paper, for which **Jon Chappell** is very grateful.

Grant Sturgis was not cheating on his wife. The white Maltese named **April** really was the pet of a colleague who had to join Grant on a last-minute business trip. The colleague's name was Bob and he occasionally wears a red wig and women's clothing.

Caroline Sturgis is still looking for her big idea and it comes in book three of the Dirty Business mystery series.

Author's Note

This is a work of fiction. There really is a state of Connecticut, a University of Connecticut, a Merritt Parkway, and a corpse flower. The corpse flower, by the way, is a magnificent plant, and if there's one blooming anywhere near you, you should check it out. Most everything else just exists between my two ears; any similarity to actual people, places, laws, tribes, etc., is purely accidental.